Ryker's War (Broken Souls Motorcycle Club)

Terri Marie Pemberton

Published by Terri Marie Pemberton, 2024.

RYKER'S WAR (BROKEN SOULS MOTORCYCLE CLUB)

First edition. December 18, 2024.

ISBN: 979-8224066414

Written by Terri Marie Pemberton.

Table of Contents

Prologue

Demi

I know I'm interrupting my bestie's moment with her man but damn they disappeared and left me with the Grinch for hours.

Serves them right if you ask me.

Settling in for a spell, I channel my fierce momma bear. With a look of mock disdain, my words to Kate are meant to incite a reaction from the man at her back.

"Personally, I think you should've made him work harder for your forgiveness. Maybe a little begging on his knees first. But that's just me. If he's what you want, I'll keep my mouth shut. For now, anyway." I throw my friend a wink her man can't see, a silent reassurance I'm not serious. At least not completely.

Giving them no time to respond, I shift my attention to the main room of the clubhouse in search of my next spiral partner.

Might as well have some fun.

"Shots!" I know my girl will refuse before I even throw my exuberant shout out into the air.

The lack of response from the entirety of the room is no shock. It also doesn't bother me one bit.

My real goal is to provoke the hot sexy leader of this group to engage with me. He took his death glare to the kitchen an hour ago like he can't stand the sight of me and that just won't do.

It's time to recapture his attention.

"Girl, I love you, but I am *not* doing shots with you again. I learned my lesson at Dean's."

Kate's reply isn't a surprise but still I play along. "Poo, you're no fun. I need someone to do shots with me!"

It's all a ploy. One meant to incite a reaction.

With no volunteers – no doubt Ryker's influence – I zero in on Bomber. The brother unlucky enough to cross my path is the perfect opportunity to stir something up.

The man whose attention I really want finally saunters in from the kitchen, stopping short in the doorway. His glare is aimed my way. Arms crossed, muscles bulging, that stern 'I'm the man in charge' countenance stamped all over his face.

Like a conquering warrior. He *knows* who he is. The power he wields.

Yummy.

Six feet plus of bulging muscles. Dark, almost midnight black hair, cut military short with just enough length on top to sink my fingers in and hold on for a ride. But it's those piercing emerald eyes that never fail to ignite a fire in my core when they lock onto mine.

Oh goodie, the man I really want to rock my world.

Don't get me wrong, he is the epitome of the perfect male specimen but his draw is so much more than his oh so delicious exterior. It's the way in which he guides his club. The obvious respect exhibited by each and every person here, reflected in every witnessed interaction since I met them all.

Earned but not commanded.

The silent power and fortitude.

That is the attraction.

He draws me in like a moth to a flame and I am so ready to feel the burn.

"Bomber! Come do a shot with me." My words may be for Bomber but my eyes are locked in a battle of wills with the glowering giant across the room.

The same man that storms my way before the words fully pass my lips.

He descends on me like an avenging angel. An irresistibly ticking bomb wrapped in denim and leather.

Stepping between us before Bomber can even acknowledge me, Ryker's fierce scowl hits me right in my girly parts. That stormily striking face hovering directly above my own brings to mind other more pleasurable activities with him poised above me in an entirely different way.

"Demi, what did I tell you about flirting with my brothers?" The pissed off man gives me no time to sass back before he bends low, putting his shoulder in my stomach.

When he straightens to his full height, I find myself a *long* way off the ground.

Not that I mind.

Not. At. All.

My eyes are riveted to the gloriously perfect ass filling my vision.

Not exactly what I was going for but I'm not complaining.

This hunk of man meat is the perfect distraction from the shit show of my life. The one I left behind in California.

I play the part, letting him think he's getting one over on me, yelling and beating away at his back as he stomps down the hallway. Not letting on he's taking me right where I want to be.

His room in the back my goal all along.

"Put me down you Neanderthal! Remember what happened the last time you manhandled me?" As usual, he ignores my rant altogether. And my fists.

Not that I'm surprised.

The man has the control of a saint. Even my knee to his junk didn't faze him the last time I pushed him to play this game with me.

The slam of the door is my first clue I may have gone a little too far this time.

In for a penny....and all that.

Blood rushes to my brain when I find myself abruptly set back on my feet. Head spinning, I cling to his biceps as my equilibrium returns. His strong muscles are a distraction as they bunch and flex in my grip. Without direction from my brain, my hands squeeze automatically. Testing the firmness. The amazing strength.

"What is wrong with you?" Ryker demands.

Clearly, he's not as distracted by our connection as I am.

It takes a willpower I didn't know I possessed to let those glorious muscles slip through my grasp.

"What do you mean? I thought you boys knew how to party and I'm looking to have a good time. What does it matter to you?" I know I'm pushing too hard.

This man has proven time and time again that he is not one to be trifled with. But I just can't help myself. I can no more control my actions around him as the air I breathe.

Doing the opposite of what I expect, he pulls away, taking two giant steps back for good measure. He stands proud in front of me, arms crossed, perma-scowl firmly in place. Nothing new there.

Ryker is the perfect picture of male dominance. Of rugged beauty.

A lesser woman might be too scared to appreciate the intimidating vision he makes.

But that just isn't me. I love testing his limits. Aiming to push him past the breaking point, where he has no choice but to let go of that tight grip on his control.

It will be a beautiful thing and I plan on being the woman lucky enough to reap the rewards when that happens.

"Demi, none of my brothers are gonna give you the good time you're looking for." His words yank me right out of my fantasy.

"Does that mean you are?" I purr.

Brows furrowed, eyes narrowed, his glacial expression could freeze the sun.

The look on his face may say my forwardness doesn't affect him but he can't do a damn thing to hide his body's reaction. The bulge behind his zipper contradicts the lie ready to fall from his lips.

This man wants me. And for whatever reason, he keeps denying my clear invitation.

Maybe he just needs a little push.

Unconsciously, I glide my hands sensually up along my sides, imagining it's him. His rough palms cupping the swell of my breasts as I push them up as an offering.

Through the layers of my clothes, my fingers close around my nipples, pinching in the way I fantasize him doing. Hungering to feel his mouth closing over the tips, teeth nibbling with just right amount of pressure.

With one step forward, he crowds me back against the door. Pressing his hard body to mine and stirring my arousal to new heights.

Much to the dismay of my body's desires, he once again does the opposite of what I want.

His hands reach up. Not to join the teasing show. Instead, he takes my wrists in a firm grip. A grip he uses to pull my own hands off my breasts.

In a move I'm achingly familiar with, he uses that hold to raise my arms until I feel the press of the unforgivingly hard wood of the door above my head. There he holds me captive, one large hand circling both of my wrists.

I'm his for the taking but I know from experience he won't give in to the desire swirling in his eyes.

His towering form is an anchor holding me in place. A glorious weight igniting a fire in my blood. He holds me captive with that electrifying gaze, the tantalizing pressure of one hard thigh fit right between the juncture of my thighs.

Apparently, he learned his lesson from the last time we played this game, keeping my lethal weapons from a repeat strike to his junk.

This is the closest we've ever been and just as erotic as I imagined it to be. The hard muscles of his thick thigh the perfect pressure on my core.

He's just as hypnotic as I fantasized.

And I won't lie, I have fantasized. Too many times to count. An embarrassing number of times alone with my vibrator.

Don't judge. Self-love is nothing to be ashamed of.

His free hand caresses down the sensitive skin of my arm, prickles of awareness left in his wake. Those tingles zip right through me like a bolt of lightning, an electric shock shot straight to my clit. My core throbs in need, rhythmic clenches searching for the fullness only he can provide. I just know he'll fill me to overflowing.

"Demi, you have nothing to prove here. No one, man or woman, in this clubhouse questions your integrity. You can be yourself, no front needed." He says.

His words are a bucket of ice to the fire in my pussy, bringing me crashing back to reality with a healthy dose of fear.

Fear that sends the organ behind my ribcage racing, a living breathing reminder that this man has the power to crush me if given half the chance.

If I give him what he's asking for.

I have no idea how this man sees through me. Sees right to the heart of me.

My insecurities.

My shortcomings.

Not only does he see them, he doesn't judge. For some reason, he has a genuine desire to understand me.

Understand what makes me tick.

And that scares the shit out of me.

No, thanks. Been there, done that. Have the scars to prove it.

Masking the urgency with which I need to escape his penetrating gaze, I put on the front everyone expects of me.

Laughing in the face of his scrutiny, I do what I do best when someone gets too close. Redirecting to deflect, I refuse to acknowledge he is getting to my truth.

"Alright, Big Guy." I say. "I get it. I'm not gonna find what I'm looking for here. You can let me go now and I'll go find what I want somewhere else."

"Don't you ever get tired of hiding yourself?" He doesn't buy it.

He never does.

He releases me, not giving me a chance to respond, inherently understanding I won't give in that easily. His expression is a mask of disappointment – with a large helping of frustration – as he puts the physical and mental distance between us that I so desperately need right now.

With one sweep of his arm to the door behind me, I'm effectively dismissed without a word.

It stings but I don't let it show. I brought this on myself with my constant refusal to give him what he wants.

Pasting on a disappointed look of my own, I grasp the door handle.

I just can't resist one last dig. "I thought you'd be more fun, Big Guy. I guess the rumors are just that. Rumors."

With that last parting shot thrown over my shoulder, I walk out the door. My head held high, a promise to myself to keep my distance from this man.

It's a necessary evil if I want to keep my secrets.

Chapter One

Demi

To say it's been a whirlwind year since I opened the doors of my bakery would be an understatement.

But my dream has become a reality in ways I could never imagine when I decided to take a chance on myself.

I'm doing what I love. Creating sweet treats – hence the name – and I'm lucky enough to have the opportunity to share those creations with other people.

People that *pay* for those treats.

The Tennessee location inspires thoughts of simple living, an idyllic reminder of life moving at a slower pace. A laidback lifestyle where people take the time to be present in the moment, not letting life get away from them.

Such a stark difference from the fast-paced world I left in California and I can honestly say I don't miss it one bit. My only regret is the family I left behind. Despite the necessity of my quick exit from their lives, I miss my mom and sisters something fierce.

Girl, you had to do what you had to do to protect them.

Kate, the absolute best thing that's happened to me since my move to Frostown – you know, aside from my bakery making a profit – sends the bell on my front door jingling to announce her arrival. She doesn't know it but she has been a lifesaver to my lonely existence here.

"Hey girl! What are you doing here?" I don't even try to mask my joy as she saunters through my front doors.

I met her one fateful morning when her curiosity got the best of her, walking into my bakery on her way to the high school and the job that made her miserable. Making that move was the best decision she ever made.

But that's just my opinion.

She would probably say it was giving her man a second chance. A decision I didn't agree with at the time but even I have to say it's been a good one for her.

Her boyfriend, Mac, is a member of the Broken Souls Motorcycle Club. The MC made the move to Frostown, building a new clubhouse on the outskirts of town not long before my arrival.

The unassuming building just outside of town is tastefully designed. Not as in your face as some other motorcycle clubs I've been in. The artful logo on the front of the building denoting it a motorcycle club the only identifying factor.

I'm sure that is all Ryker's doing. The façade of the building a reflection of the quietly stoic man who leads the club and is so highly respected by every member within the tightknit group.

Ugh girl, we've put that man out of mind, remember?

"It's been a while since I had one of your sinful croissants and I just couldn't help myself." She teases.

With perfect timing, my friend unknowingly halts my spiral down the rabbit hole that is that frustrating man.

My bestie has come a long way since I met her six months ago. The quiet wallflower has blossomed into a stunning rose.

I'd like to take all the credit – what with carefully cultivating the friendship – but even I have to admit the absolute love from her man was the key to her metamorphosis.

"Got it. One sinful delight coming right up." I promise.

My one employee is currently on break so I'm covering the front of the bakery. Sarah is a godsend I thought I'd never be lucky enough to find. The number of shit for brains I had to wade through in my search for a diamond in the rough is enough to fill your ears for years to come.

I don't know her entire story yet. She's another one as reserved as my best friend was when I first met her. But if I have one specialty – aside from my heavenly treats – it is getting to the heart of broken souls and bringing them back to life.

I'll get her there, slowly but surely.

Seconds later, Sarah rushes through the door from the back of the bakery.

Think and she shall appear.

"Sorry, I thought I timed my break for a lull in customers." That's another thing about my girl Sarah. She is always apologizing. I'm pretty sure it has something to do with that past she has yet to share.

In the three months she's been with me, she has quietly taken charge of the front of the bakery, handling the customers with a grace and patience I definitely lack.

"Sarah, I've told you time and time again, it's not a big deal. I can manage the front while you take your breaks." My words earn me a slight nod.

Like I said, I'm still working on her. She needs to learn that it is perfectly acceptable to stand up for herself. Accept the understanding and patience from others – that if I had to guess – has been lacking in her life. A softly firm touch is needed to get her there.

One I'm confident I can provide as her friend. Along with the patience of the MC family where she lives with her kids. I'm still not sure how that came about. What I do know, her and her kids, they don't belong to any of the brothers.

"The club is having a party this weekend. Are you going to show your face?" Kate, ever the empath, takes mercy on Sarah. She redirects the conversation away from the shy woman.

While not my favorite topic, I'll play along. I do not need my friend figuring out the real reason I avoid the clubhouse like the plague now.

"If there'll be fresh meat, you might be able to entice me to show up." I sass right back at her.

Her burst of laughter tells me I'm not as good of an actress as I thought.

Her words just confirm that theory. "I don't think so. Besides, even if there is, Ryker isn't going to let them anywhere near you."

And that my friends is the real reason why I keep my distance. Every interaction with that man is a direct hit to the fortress around my heart. He doesn't buy the mirage that is my defense mechanism.

"Hmm. Well then, I think I'll be busy washing my hair." I'm smart enough to avoid committing to any activities involving the man who rules my dreams. Even all these months later.

"Please Demi. Come for me?" she pouts adorably.

She's definitely learned some of my tricks.

Girl sure has learned how to work me.

But I remain strong in the face of her manipulation. "Maybe. I'll let you know later this week."

Her disappointment is clear but she gives me the obvious out. Taking her croissant, she waves goodbye after confirming that I will indeed call her later. *Sheesh, Ryker isn't the only one that sees right through me.*

Sarah follows Kate to the door, flipping the sign to closed to signal the end of the day. We spend a quiet hour cleaning and prepping the front for the next day before Sarah takes her own exit.

Chapter Two

Demi

After Sarah leaves, I spend another hour in the kitchen, prepping what I can for the following morning. The exhaustion is real by the time I drag my tired butt up the stairs to my apartment above the bakery.

The fatigue weighing on me pulls down with it the usual guard that keeps thoughts of my family from creeping in. Leaving my mom and sisters back in California, in the town I was born and raised, was one of the hardest decisions I've ever had to make.

The fact my ex escalated his harassment to threats against them when I wouldn't give him what he wanted was the final straw. The motivation I needed to make the break.

Packing my meager belongings, I drove away from Sacramento, my mom and younger sister in tears when I called to tell them I was leaving.

It was for the best.

A fact my older sister delighted in pointing out.

Bianca, three years my senior, is the oldest of mom's three girls. We always had our differences growing up, never as close as you would expect sisters so close in age to be.

Even before the threats from my ex escalated, Bianca was always my toughest critic. My boisterous personality and love of all things loud were in direct contrast to her quietly studious nature.

I consoled myself with the fact that she didn't know how to handle me. I'm an acquired taste and I just wasn't her flavor.

I tried. I really did. My mom was always begging me to make nice with her. To build a relationship with her like the one I have with my other sister Amy.

11

Amy and I are closest in age at just under two years apart. She was my partner in crime growing up. Not quite as outgoing as me but I could typically talk her into going along with my harebrained ideas.

The one she balked at – entering the lion's den of the Black Demon's MC clubhouse – was one I truly wish I had never come up with.

And the one where my troubles really started. My ex, Dwight, is a member of the sadistic club.

His ridiculous name should have been my first clue to stay away.

But I was young and fearless. Never even considering anything bad could happen to me. Assumed bad things only happened to other people.

Oh, how naïve I'd been.

A series of unfortunate events ultimately drove me to end things with him.

Or at least try to.

When I finally had enough, I flew through my apartment with fear in my heart, packing what few possessions Dwight left me. Pathetic really, how little space they took up in my car. Within an hour, I was on the highway, meandering with no destination in mind. Just me and girl power lyrics on blast to drown out my thoughts.

Five days after pulling out of my driveway for the last time, I took a look at the landscape of my surroundings. I had no idea where I was. My random cross-country trip was spent on backroads and seldom traveled highways. The signs I passed told me I had just crossed the border to Tennessee.

And then it hit me.

Who would look for me in a state so different than my home? Not quite convinced I was ready to put down roots right there, I continued heading east through the state.

The moment I crossed the Frowtown city limits, I felt like I was coming home. Not physically – Tennessee was definitely not California – but the picturesque little town was perfect.

The main street running through town – aptly named Main Street – was lined with the cutest businesses reminiscent of days gone by.

With hope in my heart, I found a non-descript hotel, dropped my meager belongings in the room I rented at a weekly rate then set out to explore the town. The people were nice as could be. A direct contrast to the horror stories I've heard from friends visiting other states.

We Californian's get a bad rep.

The vacant shop smack dab in the middle of Main Street sealed the deal. I took it as a sign of fate that it was. My dream to open my own bakery was at my fingertips.

The chime of my phone pulls me from my trip down memory lane.

Kate: So I know I said I would wait for your answer but I really want you to come to the clubhouse this weekend

Another text comes through before I can respond.

Kate: Please! We can even do a girls night next weekend. I know you've been dying to get back to Deans

Man, she's getting good at mastering the Master.

My friend has become hard to deny anything since completing her metamorphosis.

I also suspect she knows the real reason I have avoided the clubhouse all these months.

I haven't seen Ryker since that night in his room.

The night he pushed too hard.

But try as I might, he hasn't left my thoughts. Those piercing green eyes will be the death of me.

The qualities that make him such a great leader of his men are the same ones I fear will wear me down. His intensely patient approach, the understanding and empathy I recognize when I'm around him.

He *sees* me. Has since the night we met all those months ago.

He sees the flaws I mask. The insecurity I cover with my outrageous words and behavior.

When I'm with him, I *want* to give him my truth. The good, the bad and the ugly. Hand it over and let him do what he does best. Protect those he cares about.

And he does care. I know that.

Intellectually, I know he is nothing like Dwight. Ryker is an honorable man. A true leader. A man others will follow to the depths of hell if he commands it.

I long to give in to my desire.

The craving inside to hand over control. But after my ex, I don't trust my own judgement.

I just can't do it.

What I can do is be there for my friend. So, with a quiver in my fingers, I agree against my better judgement.

Me: Ok fine. You twisted my arm. I'll be there

It'll be fine. I just have to keep my distance.

Don't tempt the lion, Demi. Keep your distance and you'll survive the night. It should be simple.

Might be time for a prayer.

Chapter Three

Ryker

The main room of the clubhouse is a sight for sore eyes as I drag my tired ass onto a stool, motioning to the prospect behind the bar for a whiskey.

I feel aches in places like never before after another long ass ride back from our original charter in New Orleans.

It was my third trip down in the last two months and I'll fully admit running the two clubhouses is exhausting business.

Dime, my VP, was supposed to be the one splitting time between our clubhouses, running shit down there while I get us set up here.

But he's been on an assignment for Uncle Sam that has been extended too many times to count. The brother's been offline for almost a year and we're all getting restless about it.

Even though we've all retired from the military, the majority of the club members still do assignments when the mission calls to us on a personal level. But Dime is the one most active. I worry about my brother. Being off the grid for so long usually means shit went sideways and he doesn't have any of us there to cover his six.

The press of a soft body at my side jerks me from those worrisome thoughts. Jade grabs my attention with a side hug. "Ryker, you're back! How was the trip?"

I answer while pulling myself out of her grip. "Long fucking trip. I'm exhausted."

It's true. My bed is calling my name and I still have shit to deal with here before I can even think to answer the call.

"So, I heard a certain cute blond will be at the party tomorrow night. Kate convinced her to come." That news perks my tired body right up. That cute blond has done her best to avoid me since the night in my room here three months ago.

I know I came on too strong but damn she tests my restraint. As President of the club, I always have to be in control. In charge of the men and women that rely on my leadership to make the best decisions for our livelihoods.

I don't take that lightly. But lately, I'm looking for something more.

At thirty-four I was over the drinking, partying and sexual shenanigans. I'm ready to settle down. Maybe start a family. Have someone I can go home to every night.

The problem was I hadn't met a woman that could handle my controlling ways. The necessary rigid hold I keep on my emotions. While it was imperative in order to lead the club, unfortunately it also spilled over into my personal relationships.

What woman wants a relationship with a domineering asshole?

I wanted a woman that wasn't afraid to stand up to me. Confront my controlling ways and call me on my shit. Someone that tests the tight rein I keep on my emotions. That pushes me to let those reins go.

A woman that will walk beside me, not in the shadow of my footsteps.

An equal to lean on, in good times and bad. And I'm pretty sure I found that in Demi. The curvaceous blond may be petite – standing almost a foot shorter than my six-foot four stature – but her personality is ten feet tall.

She doesn't take my shit. She pushes my buttons, eagerly awaiting the eruption.

The problem is, she uses those methods as a self-defense mechanism. She refuses to let me in. Her sarcasm and outrageousness, her way of keeping people at a distance.

Even Kate hasn't gotten through to her true self. If she talks about her life before moving to Frostown, I'd be shocked.

Most of the club members are acutely aware of my obsession with her. Just the thought of her fries my exhausted mind. I don't have the brain power to engage in the conversational warfare talk of her always devolves into.

Dime's whereabouts a more pressing matter, I unashamedly ignore her comment about Demi. Instead switching the subject to the man I need to see to get any intel on him. "Where's Byte?"

"Probably in his room like always." No surprise there. The brother rarely makes an appearance outside that room.

"Thanks Jade. I'll see ya tomorrow." I tell her.

"Night Ryker." She calls out.

Tapping my knuckles on the bar top, I force my tired body to my feet to go in search of him.

Unsurprisingly his door is shut tight when I trudge down the hall. Not giving a shit if he's asleep, I bang my fist on his door, then wait impatiently for it to open.

He doesn't disappoint as the door swings open a minute later. "Sup Prez?"

His look is unique to an MC. Black rimmed glass, slicked back hair and slim build. All are more the markers of corporate America. The cut he wears proudly contradicts his clean-cut appearance. He may be Ivy league educated but don't let that fool you. The man is deadly and not only with a computer.

"You heard from Dime?" If anyone could find info on the MIA brother, Byte is the man to do it.

"Naw, man. I haven't heard anything from him." He says.

My dread increases. Dime is well aware he's supposed to keep Byte updated on his whereabouts. If Byte hasn't heard from him, the brother must be in deep. Or in deep shit.

"Can you find him?" I try to keep the distress out of my voice. From the look on his face, I am nowhere near successful. The exhaustion is real, breaking down the tight leash I usually have on my emotions.

"I'll see what I can do. Let you know what I find." He says.

"Thanks brother. I'm gonna head to my room." I'm dead on my feet.

"You're staying here?" He asks.

The question isn't surprising. It's not often I stay at the clubhouse anymore. Most nights I end up riding the five miles further outside of town to my lake house.

I just don't have it in me tonight. My ass would protest planting it back on my bike after the long ass ride from New Orleans.

"Yeah. I'm too tired to ride home tonight. See ya in the morning." I tell him before heading to my room.

I drag my tired body into the shower, washing the dirt and grime of the road away. Stumbling out of the bathroom, I collapse face down in my king size bed at long last, not even bothering to remove my towel.

As it always does when I lay my head down, my mind goes back to a particular curvy blond who continuously dominates my dreams.

My last thought before sleep takes me is whether or not she'll show up for the party tomorrow night. I sure am looking forward to the fireworks if she does.

***

Back at the bar after a much-needed night of sleep, I'm ruminating on how to get Demi to drop her guard and open up to me.

I throw back my glass of whiskey while keeping an eye on the door. Annoyed with myself, I turn away, feeling like a preteen obsessed with my first crush.

Jade sure isn't helping. She's been glued to my side since I sat at the bar, taking the opportunity to sing Demi's praises enthusiastically as usual.

"She's a take charge kind of woman. Just what you need to keep you on your toes." With how she's going on, you would think Jade has a thing for Demi herself.

Nodding, I tune out her opinion on the perfect woman for me.

She isn't telling me anything I haven't told myself in the late hours of the night when Demi dominates my dreams.

I won't even guess how many times I've woken up with my hand wrapped around my cock, ready to blow. An embarrassing number of times. That's all I'm gonna say. Her fiery nature so much of a turn on it physically hurts sometimes.

I turn on my barstool, swiveling around to survey the main room. The predictable debauchery does nothing to catch my interest.

I haven't partaken in the sexual activities in well over a year. No woman has stirred my cock since the night I set eyes on Demi at Dean's Bar. Truthfully, I lost interest in the meaningless sex long before that night.

At this stage of my life, I'm more interested in quality over quantity.

Best to leave the shameless shenanigans to the younger brothers who aren't looking for anything serious just yet.

Eyes still pathetically glued to the door, I clock her the second she walks in with Kate at her side. A sinful red dress graces her curves, sensually conforming to her body like a second skin just the way my hands itch to do.

The skirt ends in a teasing whisper high on her firm thighs. All that supple flesh on display for every motherfucker here to see.

The blood red color matches the stain on her lips, igniting fantasies of those plump lips wrapped around my cock. A cock that didn't react at all to the debauchery, now swells to full hardness as I take her in.

I'm not surprised by her wardrobe choice. Demi is always looking to stand out in the crowd. The woman doesn't know how to blend into the background.

It's just another piece of her personality that intrigues me.

Let the fireworks begin.

Chapter Four

Demi

I should be ready and waiting for Kate to pick me up already. Instead, I continue the search for the perfect outfit to leave one infuriating club president drooling.

Honestly, I really can't find it in myself to care if I miss the party tonight. I'm more concerned with avoiding the sexy man that consumes my thoughts. Doesn't mean I don't want to look hot in my avoidance.

If Kate is gonna guilt me into going to this party – and really I don't want to let her down – I plan to knock it out of the park. Or him off his feet. I'll take either outcome at this point. Nothing less than irresistible is acceptable tonight to show that jerk exactly what he turned down.

The big guy won't know what hit him.

I find what I'm looking for in the very back of my closet. The little red dress has been waiting for just the right occasion to hug my curves.

Tonight is the perfect night to put this little gem on display. Pairing it with black heels to give me some much-needed inches and red lipstick that is a perfect match to the dress. I decide to leave my hair in its naturally loose waves down my back.

As a baker, I don't have much of an opportunity to let it loose so my head thanks me for avoiding the tight bun I usually subject it to. Even though all that weight piled on top of my head is heavy, I don't have it in me to part with any of the length.

With perfect timing, I hear Kate's honk right as I give myself one last look in the mirror.

Eat your heart out, Big Guy.

Tossing my essentials in a seldom used clutch, I head downstairs to meet my friend. Her car idles in a spot right in front of the bakery, the street empty at this time of the night.

As I slide into the passenger seat, her gawking stare confirms I have indeed accomplished my goal.

"Wow, Demi. The brothers won't be able to take their eyes off you in that dress." Awe fills her voice.

"Perfect. That is exactly what I was going for." I sass.

The response is routine, the outrageousness exactly what I typically pull out with others. Yet it gets harder every day to keep my secrets from my best friend. She's become like another sister, even closer than Amy and I have always been.

But I worry about blowback from my not so distant past. If anything came back on Kate, I wouldn't be able to live with myself. So, I keep my self-imposed isolation firmly in place.

"Let's do this!" With a laugh to cover my morose thoughts, I prompt her to get the car on the road.

I've become the queen of deflection.

As she reverses out of the parking spot, a giggle bursts from past her lips as she turns the car in the direction of the Broken Souls clubhouse.

We chat on the drive. I make a point to ask leading questions meant to keep the focus on my friend.

This is such an exciting time for Kate. She's working close with Ryker and her man, Mac, to get a shelter up and running in the old hotel down the road from the clubhouse. Finally stepping out the shadow of her father's expectations, the MC has given her the chance to make her own dreams come true.

If there is one thing I admire about Ryker, his tenacity in the face of something he wants is almost irresistible. Sadly, it is a double edged sword when it comes to me, so worried that same tenacity will lead to his demise.

While the men of the club renovate the abandoned hotel, Kate works fulltime to vet the staff hired for her shelter, while simultaneously working on expanding the services she offers in the community. Even though she's super busy, my bestie glows with the happiness of following her heart.

The drive flies by as she chatters excitedly and before I'm quite ready, we sit in front of the clubhouse. My observant friend recognizes my nerves, giving me a minute to compose myself before prompting me out of the car.

"Ready?" She asks. "Mac said they have some brothers visiting from New Orleans, so it'll probably be packed tonight."

Oh goodie. Let's hope Ryker is too busy to find me.

Walking through the doors of the clubhouse, the sensual beat of the music vibrates through me. My body buzzes with the excitement of the sensual displays all around us.

Kate leans over to whisper in my ear. "Behave. I'm serious about all the men watching you. Ryker isn't going to be happy." Seems my friend knows me well.

I throw my head back, a carefree laugh breaking free, brushing off her worry while we navigate the crowded room to the bar. My smile slips when I notice Ryker is already there, a hungry gleam in his eyes, almost as if he was eagerly anticipating my arrival.

Stumbling at the thought, I barely catch myself at the intensity in those shocking emerald eyes.

So much for avoiding the enticing man.

Girl, pull up your big girl panties.

"Hey, Big Guy. You been hiding from me? I haven't seen you around lately." I use my usual sarcasm to keep him at bay. Maybe a heavy dose of attitude will discourage him.

I have no problem with the lie. He doesn't need to know I'm the one taking the avoidance route.

But he sees right through my bullshit. That hawk-like gaze caught my stumble even as the rest of the room missed it. I can see it in his eyes but for some reason he plays along.

"I've been busy. The way you leave me with blue balls every time you walk away, I've had to give my cock a break from you." He taunts.

Well damn, that sure is a depressing thought. I might avoid him like the plague but that doesn't mean I have any desire to hear about him with other women.

"Hmm, so you've been keeping the ladies busy?" The question slips free before I can censor myself.

Way to show your hand dummy.

I just can't help it, I am a glutton for punishment.

He takes pity on me – I'm not that great an actress so I'm sure my disappointment shows on my face – quick to clarify.

"No Demi." He says. "I've been crystal clear. The only lady I want to keep me busy is you."

Not giving me a second to dwell on that revelation, he stands. Towering over me, he extends his hand. Almost as if he's made a decision and that decision is in direct opposition of my goal to avoid him.

"Dance with me." It's not really a question.

Probably because he knows I would refuse if it was. He takes possession of my hand, leading me to the crowded dance floor.

I'd have to be dense to miss his blatant stamp of ownership. He might as well mark his territory with the way he glares at every other man in the room. The 'keep your eyes to yourself' message clear for all to see.

The feel of his body overwhelms my senses when he pulls me close. My hands clench involuntarily where they rest on his chest at the feel of his strong thigh slipping between my own. The hard muscles of his pecs flex beneath my palms. His strong arm wraps around my waist to pull me impossibly closer.

Even in heels, my head barely reaches his shoulder.

I feel safe.

Protected.

Completely unfamiliar territory for me.

No man has ever made me feel this way.

Shivers skate down my spine when I *feel* him take a deep inhale of the sensitive skin of my neck. Shivers that are impossible to miss.

"What are you doing, Ryker?" My voice is wary.

With one more deep inhale, he raises his head, making sure to snag my gaze before speaking. "I want you, Demi."

Not this again.

"You had your chance, remember?" I remind him. "I've offered myself to you an embarrassing number of times. You always turn me down."

"You know I want more than your body." He reminds me.

And that right there is what I'm afraid of.

Rather than allowing him to pull me into the usual tedious argument, I let down my guard. Bask in the moment, promising myself this is temporary. Soon I'll step away. Rebuild the walls around my heart.

But in this moment, pressed close to his tantalizing body, the sensual music weaves a spell around us. The same as the provocative magic he inspires with his natural grace.

Our bodies sway together in a hedonistic dance. He's breaching my defenses, igniting the desire only he can. Shredding my self-control until I'm a jumbled mass of desire, overwhelmed by the intoxicating scent and feel that is all Ryker.

The scene around us doesn't help. Everywhere my eyes stray, there are people in varying stages of sexual activity. Dana dances to my left, her top gone as she sways unabashedly between Rocker and a man I don't recognize.

I watch in captive intrigue as the two men tease her mercilessly, an illicit display that has wetness escaping to soak my thong.

Cheers from the bar tear my captivated eyes from the threesome lost in their own world. Going up on the tips of my toes, I peek over Ryker's shoulder to see Mac holding my friend in his arms, her legs locked around his waist as he kisses the hell out of her. She pulls back to pepper kisses all over his face.

"Looks like Mac finally popped the question." My gaze flies up to Ryker's to find his not on the scene at the bar but instead searing down into mine.

"What?" I gasp.

That jackass.

I had no idea he was even considering asking my friend to marry him. He definitely should have run that by me. I would have helped him plan the shit of that.

And definitely not during a club party.

But even as the indignation hits me, there is no way to miss the happiness on my friend's face. Even I can see this is perfect for the two of them.

Ryker tightens his hold when I attempt to disengage, intent on congratulating the happy couple. To join the celebration.

"Give me a chance, Demi." He says. "You know we could be great together."

He just doesn't give up. But then, I'm a stubborn pain in the ass myself.

"I don't know that." I deny. "I don't know you, Ryker. Not really."

"Then spend time with me. Just the two of us. Get to know me." He presses.

Turmoil rages in my belly. This man has the power to break me. He says he's into me but how long will that last when he learns about my past? The bad decisions I made with a shady MC. One that scares the shit out of me to this day.

Why do you keep denying me?" He breaks through my inner turmoil.

Not up for another mental battle with this man, I step out of his arms. "I'll think about it, Big Guy." I hedge as I move around him to head to the bar.

I'm getting way too good at that.

It's the best I can do at this point. He's wearing me down and I'm downright scared of what will happen when he finally breaks through.

Wading through the crowd, I make my way to the celebration at the bar to drag my friend into a tight hug when I finally reach the happy couple.

"Kate! You little devil! Why didn't you tell me this was happening?" I tease.

Face glowing with the happiness she has no hope of hiding – and why would she even want to – she returns my hug with a watery laugh.

"Demi! I had no idea Mac was planning this." Her words overflow with her excitement.

"I'm so happy for you, friend. He's a lucky man." Squeezing her tighter, my whisper lacks my usual sarcasm.

With the sentimentality out of the way, we spend the rest of the night celebrating. Kate even going so far as doing a couple of shots with me before Mac cuts her off.

The night becomes a blur as I throw back shots in the happy couple's honor.

Waking up alone in my bed the next morning, I have no clue how I got home. Or if I even spoke to Ryker again last night.

I bury my pounding head in my pillow and do what I do best – put the question out of mind.

What I don't know can't hurt me and all that.

Chapter Five

Demi

I eventually drag my hungover self out of bed later that afternoon, the mystery of how my night ended still unsolved.

The struggle is real.

After a cup of coffee to clear the cobwebs, I decide to bury my head – and hands – in cleaning supplies and go to work on my bathroom. The tediously hard work always clears my head and right now I need the good ole fashioned distraction to figure out my shit.

I have no idea what to do about Ryker. Or if I already made a decision last night.

Those damn shots turned my head to a mass of fuzzy flashes. But when I try to capture any of those short clips, they float just out of my grasp.

The only one with some clarity is grinding on someone on the dance floor after my fifth – okay maybe sixth – shot.

Knowing the control freak that Ryker is, I have to assume it was his body I was using to show off my awesome stripper moves.

Let's be real here. When the shots start flowing, I channel my best Magic Mike moves. What seems like a good idea with some alcohol becomes cringe worthy in the light of day – and sobriety.

Thankfully, a ring from my phone draws me out of those embarrassing speculations.

My sister's name on the caller ID obliterates all relief at the distraction. Instead replaced with the same distress I suffer with every call from California.

Worry mounts. Amy wouldn't call without a damn good reason. I yank off my rubber gloves and answer on the second ring. "Amy, what's wrong?"

"Demi, you have to come home. Mom had a heart attack. She's in the hospital." I can barely make out her words through her tears but I hear enough to freeze my blood.

A powerful fear takes root.

Being so far from home, there is always a risk that I won't be close enough if something were to happen. But the thought never crossed my mind that a health issue would be the reason for this feeling of helplessness.

"Is she okay?" I demand.

"The doctor wants to keep her for a few days for observation." Amy evades. "They're still determining the cause and whether or not she'll need surgery."

My mom is too young for something like this to happen to her. She had all three of us girls by the time she was twenty-three years old. There is no way an active, healthy fifty-year-old woman should be going through this.

My mind hyper focused on my family, I don't even consider the consequences of my next words. All I know is I have to be there for my mom. "I'll be there as soon as I can."

"Thank God-" Whatever else she was about to say is cut off. All that comes through the speaker is muffled bickering, most likely due to the hand she must have placed over the phone. From the few words I do catch, it sounds like the familiar tones of Amy and Bianca arguing.

And shocker, Bianca doesn't want me anywhere near them.

That hurts. It really does. Not that I'm surprised.

While a small part of me understands her concern, the way my mind is spinning right now, the only thing I'm focused on is being there for Mom and Amy.

Screw Bianca!

"Amy!" I yell to stop the familiar argument.

From the deafening silence on the other end of the phone, it's obvious I interrupted them. "Amy, tell Bianca I'll be there. I don't care what she says, I need to be there for mom too."

I'm over their bickering. I have a million things to take care of before catching a flight and I'm already looking at six or seven hours of travel time. I need to get off the phone to make arrangements.

Everything else can be coordinated on the way to the airport.

Fighting tears at the predicable ways of my oldest sister, I salvage my composure enough to promise to send Amy my flight info when I have it.

I hang up then quickly open my airline app and book a flight leaving in three hours.

I call Sarah, multitasking while frantically tossing clothes and necessities into a suitcase, hoping she'll agree to cover the bakery in my absence.

She picks up on the third ring, the sound of childish giggles echoing in my ear.

"Hey Demi. Sorry, the kids are on a sugar rush. *Someone* thought it would be a good idea to give them cake before naptime." She gripes.

I can't help the laugh that escapes, her irritation is obvious and I'm fairly sure that *someone* is Joker.

And the kids love him.

I've learned enough to know he's not their bio dad, but you would never know from watching him with them. He brings them to the bakery a couple times a week to visit Sarah and the bond between them is devastating to any woman's libido.

Switching back to the reason I called, I quickly make my request. "Would you mind running the bakery for a few days? I have a family emergency I need to go home for. I'm not sure how long I'll be gone."

After a beat of silence, she responds hesitantly. "Are you sure you want me to run the bakery?"

If I wasn't so caught up in my emotional frenzy, I would totally give her a lecture on self-esteem. And the fact that I have all the faith she is fully capable of holding down the fort without issue.

"Yes, Sarah. I want you to run the bakery. It's only a couple days, three tops. I just...I just really need to get home to check on my mom." At this point, I'm choking back tears again. It is absolutely unfathomable to even consider the possibility of losing my mom.

I won't let myself go there.

She's quick to agree, probably has something to do with the huskiness in my voice. I give her a rundown on what to do with opening and closing the bakery and how to prepare the pre-made pastries stored in the cooler. When I'm done giving her instructions, I hang up quickly to avoid any probing questions with the weak excuse I have a flight to catch.

Deciding it is definitely in my best interest to text Kate rather than call, I tap out a short message to let her know I'll be out of town for a few days and I'll catch her up when I return.

Cowardly I know but my bestie is far too perceptive. She won't let me off the hook as easily as Sarah did.

Before I know it, I'm at the airport with time to spare, mind spiraling as I wait for the boarding call for my plane.

And *not* in the fun way.

Chapter Six

Demi

What feels like an eternity later, my plane touches down at the international airport in Sacramento. I grab a rideshare from there and head directly to the hospital. The passing scenery shows not much has changed in the year since I left.

The urban city in no way compares to the untouched beauty of Tennessee.

The driver pulls to a stop outside Sacramento General Hospital in the heart of California's state capital. The trip only takes about fifteen minutes, traffic not too bad at this time of day.

Amy's latest text assures me Mom is holding stable in intensive care, so I hop on the elevator to the fourth floor. The nurse's station is impossible to miss when I spill out with my carry-on.

The friendly smile of the nurse manning the desk is a balm to my ragged emotions as I reach the end of my frazzled journey at last.

"Hi. My mom was admitted for a heart attack. My sister said she's still in ICU but I don't know what room she's in." I tell her.

"Sure, sweetie. What's your mom's name?" She asks.

"Demi!" Amy's voice cuts in as she comes around the corner, picking up speed before she knocks into me like an Indy car racer.

Her enthusiastic greeting is nothing compared to the death grip of her arms around me.

My attempt to pull free is futile, she just squeezes me tighter even as I fight to breathe.

Who needs air, right?

Needing the comfort as much as she does, I stop trying to escape and wrap my arms around her too.

"Amy, how is she?" I gasp out.

She pulls back to meet my eyes, answering with a sob. "The doctor says a blood clot caused the heart attack, so they put her on medication to dissolve it. They don't think she's going to need surgery but she has to stay here for a couple days."

Thank God for that.

"Am I allowed to see her?" I ask.

Amy let's her disbelief show when she finally releases her hold on me. "Of course, you can. That's not even a question."

"Hmm." I don't say what I'm really thinking but I'm sure if Bianca had her way, I wouldn't even be allowed through the door.

Not in the mood to air our dirty laundry with an audience, I wrap a hand around the handle of my suitcase and grab Amy's hand with the other.

"Come on. Lead the way." I tell her.

Dragging me around the corner where she came from, Amy leads me to a room two doors down. I take a minute to compose myself for Mom's sake before entering the room.

"Demi, baby, you're here." Mom says when she sees me lurking in the doorway.

Looking better than expected, she sits upright in the bed with wires running up out of her hospital gown. The steady beep of the heart monitor does more to reassure me than any words Amy could have possibly given me before I walked in that room.

"Mom. I missed you." My own sob bursts free before I can contain it.

I do my best to fight back tears as my feet carry me across the room, completely ignoring Bianca's glower from the chair next to the hospital bed. I catch myself just before I crash into her, gently placing my arms around her.

"Hey, none of that. I'm fine." She reassures me as her hand rubs up and down my back soothingly.

As I breathe in the familiar scent of home, the tears run freely down my cheeks. It has been *way* too long since I've had a mom hug. Guilt is all-consuming when I admit my bad decisions put us in this position to begin with.

It has *always* been the four of us against the world. Ever since our dad died when Amy was a baby, Mom has been our rock. Raising us girls to rule the world and take no shit from anyone.

It's laughable how far I fell from expectations. Running from a psychotic ex, unable to see my family, I have no one to blame but myself.

"You shouldn't have come here." Bianca intrudes on our moment.

And cue the judgement from the peanut gallery.

"Stop Bianca. Demi has as much right to be here as you do." Mom steps in just like she always does.

I pull back to really study her face, giving her a good long look.

"You look good, Mom. I missed you." I tell her.

Her own tears run down her face as she gives me a critical look of her own. No doubt noticing the changes since the last time I saw her. Bags under my eyes from my frantic cross-country trek. I've lost weight. The stress of the past year really taking its toll.

"Baby, you're skin and bones. You need to take better care of yourself." Mom admonishes.

Already shaking my head, I give her a watery smile. "Mom, I'm fine. How are you feeling?"

"I'm good. Ready to blow this joint." She jokes.

Leave it to her to gloss over the fact she had a *heart attack* like it's no big deal.

"Amy said you don't need surgery. How long do you have to stay here?" I ask.

"The doctor said a couple of days but I'm hoping to be out of here tomorrow."

"Mom, you need to listen to the doctors. We can't be having anything else happening to you." I keep it light, even though the thought of losing her terrifies me. If I let my mind go there, I'll really break down and that just wouldn't be a pretty sight.

Mom yawns, long and loud. She needs to rest, so I lean forward to press a kiss to her forehead.

"You need to sleep so you can get better all the faster. I'm going to have Amy take me back to the house. I am in desperate need of a shower but I'll be back as soon as I can." I promise.

Her lack of a comeback is more telling than anything else. Proof I made the right call as she presses a button to recline the bed.

"Come on, Demi. Let's get you to the house." Following Amy from the room, I'm not surprised in the least when Bianca is right on our heels.

"Demi, you need to leave. You're putting Mom in danger just by being here." The stab to the heart shouldn't hurt. Nor should it surprise me, Bianca is never short on hurtful words aimed to strike the deadliest.

"Relax, Big Sis. I'll be out of your hair in no time. I'm only here for a couple of days to make sure Mom's okay. I'm sure I'm not even a blip on the radar for Dwight after this long." I say the words but I'm not so sure I believe them myself.

If I know one thing about my ex, it is that he is absolutely relentless when he wants something. Add to that the fact that I escaped unscathed once before, I'm sure he's out for my blood.

I don't need to say any of that. It's clear from the look on Bianca's face she's of the same opinion.

"Just go." I'm stunned by her restraint. She holds back the words I can see on the tip of her tongue.

With a sharp nod, I turn back to Amy who has been anxiously watching the exchange.

"Let's go Amy." I say. "I really do need that shower."

Chapter Seven

Ryker

Back stiff after hours spent hunched over the desk in my office, I sit back to survey the man and woman in front of me. Kate has come a long way in the time we've worked to get her safe haven up and running.

The renovations to the hotel are almost complete. Every single member of the club has stepped up to help, volunteering their time to get the place ready as quickly as possible.

Joker has been the one most closely involved, right there every step of the way to help Kate in any way he can. They've formed an unlikely friendship over the last several months. You'll often find them joking and bickering like brother and sister.

Joker's interest in the shelter isn't surprising. We came in contact with the woman he's infatuated with during a recent investigation in a shitty situation. Sarah's husband, along with his cousin, were selling drugs from here to Redford with no care as to who bought their product. One of their customers was a student at the school the cousin worked at that tragically overdosed from their deadly product.

Sarah and her kids had nowhere to go when we helped her escape her douchebag husband after he knocked her around, so we moved them into the clubhouse. Not an ideal solution but it was the only option at the time to keep them safe.

They moved in and I haven't heard a word about her leaving. There's also the fact that Joker would kill anyone dumb enough to try to take them out of here.

On top of that, he's made it his life's mission to ensure there is a safe place for people in similar situations to land for help.

I cut into their sibling banter when it becomes apparent we're done for the day. They way they're bickering, I'm not getting any more work out of these two.

"Alright guys, good work. Assuming everything goes as planned, we should be able to open next month." I appreciate everything they've done more than I could ever say.

"Thanks, Ryker. You don't know how much this means to me." Kate's beaming smile is contagious as she stands to gather her things.

"I do, Kate." I say. "And I'm glad we're almost to the finish line. Have you had any luck with interviews? We'll need staff ready to start when we open our doors."

"There are a few potential candidates that I think will be awesome. Byte is doing background checks on them now. I'll let you know before making a final decision." She promises.

"Sounds good." I tell her.

The vibration of Kate's phone distracts her as we exit my office. There is only one person that can put that melancholy look on her face and she's currently at college hundreds of miles away.

"Is that April?" I ask.

Her fingers fly across her screen even as she gives me a quick nod. "Yes. She's trying to convince me to let her move home. Says she isn't happy living on campus."

April leaving was hard on Kate, mostly because it was obvious she was conflicted about going. Mac and the ladies of the club helped Kate convince her to spread her wings. From the sound of it, it may not be going as well as we all hoped.

Mac moved in with Kate after April left. While the change has been good for Kate, I think it's made the move harder for April. Fear of missing out most likely. Add in the fact that Mac and April grew so close before her move, sounds to me like April is really missing them both.

"Give her some time." I tell her. "She's only been there a few months. She's still adjusting. Missing you and Mac. That's all."

"That's what I keep telling her." She says. "But it's not the answer she wants to hear."

"Maybe you and Mac should take a trip to go up and visit her." I suggest.

"We're considering it. I think we might go up over the long weekend in a couple weeks." Her indecision is clear.

On the one hand, it would be good for the cousins to see each other. But then again, Kate wouldn't want to set April back if she's made some strides adjusting to her new situation.

"She'll be fine, Kate." I promise her. "It would probably do you both some good to see each other."

When we reach the main room, Kate gives us a wave as she makes her way over to her fiancé. Mac's proposal last weekend may have been a shock to Kate but for the rest of us, it was a long time coming. It is plain as day how much he loves her. If it was up to him, she would already have his last name and a baby on the way.

I drop my tired ass on a stool at the bar and wave to the prospect for a whiskey. Joker surprises me when he sits on his own stool at my side.

"Where's Sarah?" I ask. "She's usually back by this time of day."

With her part-time schedule, Sarah is typically here to spend the afternoons with her kids. The ladies of the club take turns babysitting but she feels guilty not paying them. Not that they mind, every person in the club loves those kids.

"Demi had some kind of family emergency. So Sarah's running the bakery for a few days. I'm gonna pick her up after she closes for the day." He says.

"What kind of emergency?" I ask.

Now I feel like an asshole, assuming she was avoiding me again. I didn't even stop to question why she hasn't been around the last few days.

"She didn't give Sarah any details. Just called and asked her to run the bakery. Said she'd be gone three days tops." He says.

"When did this happen?" I have a burning need to know when she'll be back. Hell, I'm an asshole for not even knowing she left.

Over the last year, I've fought all my natural instincts – and curiosity – and given Demi her privacy.

Now, I'm kicking my own ass for not knowing more. Not looking into her background.

The faith that she'll come to me in her own time isn't doing me a damn bit of good right now.

"Couple days ago. She called Sarah this morning and said she should be back by tomorrow night." Joker says, interrupting my internal berating.

"So, she doesn't know where she went for this emergency?" I press.

"Naw man, just that it had to do with her family."

I ruminate on that. There's not much I can do unless I have Byte do a background check on her. Waiting – not something I'm used to – doesn't sit well with me.

I'll give her another day but if she's not back, she isn't giving me much of a choice.

"How's Sarah handling it?" Changing the subject to exactly what I know will light my brother up, I listen with half an ear as he rattles on about Sarah's greatness.

Brother has it bad for this one.

I cut him off when he moves on to what an amazing mother she is, curious how long she'll let him keep her and the kids here. "Has she said anything about moving out of the clubhouse?"

"She isn't going anywhere, Prez." From the glower he throws my way, I get the feeling this isn't the first time the topic has come up and he doesn't seem too happy about it.

"Has she brought it up to you?" I ask.

"Yes." He answers begrudgingly. "And I'll tell you the same damn thing I told her. There is no way in hell I'm letting them go."

Well shit, it sounds like this is an argument that has been going on for a while.

"Brother, you're not gonna get anywhere with her if that's how you're telling her you want her to stay." I impart some wisdom on the dense brother.

"What am I supposed to do, Prez? We're not all like you. Thinking ten steps ahead and all that shit. I can't think beyond the fact that she wants to leave me." The insecurity driving his actions is obvious in that admittance.

At least, it is to me. Probably just sounds like an asshole to the woman he wants to convince to stay.

I slap him on the back tend put my two cents on the table. "Joker, man, you can't keep clipping her wings. She had that shit with her douchebag husband and look where it left her. You want a future with her and those kids? You give her the freedom to fly. Help her regain her confidence. Her independence. Be the man there whenever she's ready to land."

Sound advice I should be taking my damn self.

I give him another slap on the back along with one last word of advice. "Patience, brother. I know it's not your strong suit but you gotta trust this is a necessary journey for her. All you can do is make sure she knows you'll be there waiting when she's ready to land."

Now if I can just follow my own damn advice and be as patient with my own woman.

Chapter Eight

Demi

I collapse on my bed after a whirlwind three days. Frustration and worry eating away as I stare up at the ceiling, Bianca's parting shots to stay away when they dropped me at the airport set on replay. My eldest sister sure packs a punch but she's not wrong. The threat is all too real and I couldn't live with myself if anything happened to them.

Sleep eludes me as I stress about the deadly side effects my trip could have. Will Dwight find me? Is he even still looking for me? Logic says it's been so long, he probably let me go by now, but fear for my family warns me not to become complacent.

My exhaustion leaves my mind vulnerable to the memories I usually keep locked down – allowing the nightmare to creep back in.

That fateful night I entered the lion's den is as clear in my mind today as when it happened. The night I first met Dwight. One of the hottest guys in the room, he zeroed in on me as soon as I walked through the door.

The charm and good looks made it easy for him to play my naïve self. To manipulate me exactly where he wanted me. I was hooked from the jump and he played the part well. Extravagant dates. Flowers and gifts. He went all out to reel me in.

Playing the long game, I didn't even recognize the control he was slowly taking over my life until it was too late. He cut me off from my friends. Tried to do the same with my family. Thankfully, Mom and Amy were persistent. They remained stubborn in their pursuit to contact me even with him controlling every aspect of my life. Nothing was off limits to him.

The final straw was the first time his fist actually connected with my face. Before that, it was just a threat. An abstract action I never believed him capable of.

My ass was out the door fast, assuming the words "we're done" were enough to get him out of my life.

Boy was I wrong.

I learned quick he doesn't like the word no, and so my nightmare began.

At first, it was just random things. Mysterious gifts with no name. Phone calls from unknown numbers – heavy breathing in my ear. The following month, it was notes on my car. Things like "you're beautiful" and "I caught a glimpse of you today". All unsigned of course.

And then the break ins. Breaking into my car to leave me flowers and extravagant gifts but the final straw was the break in at my home. My safe haven was safe no more.

He must have been watching me, my phone ringing right as I walked through the front door. I knew it was him, his gloating voice, the sick satisfaction. His smug victory all too clear at the exact moment I caught a glimpse of the destruction of my home.

What I came to understand in that moment was he thrived on the fear. Relished in the chaos of my emotions as fear skittered down my spine. His words a promise that he would come for my family next if I didn't return to him.

I didn't think. I moved on autopilot through my once safe home, packing what little was left and calling my mom on the way out of town.

Thankfully, she was with my sisters. They were unharmed. Concern laced their words as they tried to talk me out of my hasty decision.

Well, Mom and Amy did anyway. Bianca couldn't wait a minute to tell me I told you so.

Gotta love having your mistakes thrown in your face.

Even though Bianca couldn't wait to kick my ass out of the house and back on a plane this morning, Amy promised to call if anything changed with Mom. It had to be enough for now, I couldn't take a chance with their safety.

My last thought before sleep takes me under surprisingly isn't how much I need my best friend because really, I do. But the person my heart longs for in this moment of weakness? One strong club president. A man who would move mountains to solve all my problems.

Not for the first time, I wish I had the courage to reach out for him. To let him carry my burden on those ridiculously strong shoulders.

Chapter Nine

Demi

The early morning calm of the bakery is just what my exhausted mind needs to recharge this morning. With a press of my finger, music pours from my phone as I pull out the ingredients to start on my sinful creations.

I'm in a groove, taking no notice of the sun rising in the background until an alarm from my phone warns that it's time to open the doors.

On time as usual, Sarah breezes through the door just as I turn off my tunes. "Welcome back, Demi. Is everything okay with your family?"

She's such a sweetheart. It's no wonder I was smitten as soon as I met her.

"Yes. Thanks for asking. Everything is as good as can be expected."

I'm not ready to spill about my previous life so I change the subject. "Did you have any issues while I was gone?"

"No issues. We missed you though. I'm glad you're back." She says. "I don't know how you do it. Working these long hours is rough."

"You do what you gotta do." I laugh. "It becomes second nature after a while."

"Well, I'm glad you're back." There is a whole lotta relief in her voice. "This place just isn't the same without you. Do you need any help back here before I open the doors?"

I wave her away. "No, I'm good. Go ahead and let the savages through the door."

Her tinkling laugh precedes her exit to do just that. I'm happy to say that sound is coming easier and easier these days.

I place the last tray of muffins in the oven before grabbing the cooled croissants to carry them through to the front display case.

It sure is nice to see a line has formed since Sarah unlocked the doors. She moves quickly around the counter to efficiently serve the customers as usual.

We work in harmony as I slide the tray of croissants smoothly into the display case alongside all the other sweet goodies I created this morning.

"Good morning, Mrs. Riley." I greet one of my longtime customers. Granted it's only been about six months but this town is nothing if not stuck in its ways, so it took some time for folks to warm up to the new shop in town.

And me.

Okay, mostly me. I'm definitely not the vision of the homegrown Frostown-er but they've slowly come around.

Kate has been a huge help in that department. Everyone around town loves her and her selfless support for those in need. The friendship she bestowed on me has definitely helped others warm up to me.

Speak of the devil, Kate skips through the door with her usual cheer. "Demi! You're back. I missed you. Is everything okay at home?"

This is what I love about her. She is the most genuinely nice person I have ever met in my life.

I move around the counter to wrap her in a hug, missing my bestie as much as she missed me. "Girl, I missed you too! Everything is fine or it will be." I keep my voice low for her ears only.

We have an audience. No surprise there. Every person in the shop is shamelessly ear hustling.

Gotta love small towns.

"Do you need anything?" She asks with a soft smile. "You know I'm here for you. You don't have to take on the world by yourself."

Her words leave me fighting tears.

Stupid emotions.

Other than Mom and Amy, no one else has been there to offer support with no strings. Kate is the most selfless person I have met in my life. I don't know what I would have done without her in this small town, so foreign to where I grew up.

"No, really. I'm fine." I eventually answer her question. "Do you have time to hang out this morning? I can meet you at our table once the morning rush passes."

"Of course. I made sure to make time to catch up this morning." She leaves me at the counter to take a seat at our usual table.

The morning rush passes quickly. Sarah is amazing in her own right, handling the customers with ease. After an hour of rushing from back to front to refill the quickly dwindling pastry case, I finally get a chance to take a break and plop down in the chair across from my bestie.

From what I can see, she's knee deep in plans for her dream.

"How are things going at the hotel? Are all the renovations done?" I ask.

"We're getting there. Ryker has a few final touches he asked for, so Joker and I have been making some final adjustments to the plans." She says while putting her paperwork away.

Well damn. I hoped we could at least get through catching up before *his* name came up. Even with the drama and worry of my visit home, that man was never far from my thoughts.

"Sarah did a great job running the bakery while I was gone. I came in early to get caught up and there was nothing for me to do but jump right back into creating more goodies." I won't lie, I'll avoid the shit out of the topic of that man.

"That's what Joker said. He sure wasn't happy with the hours she was working. I think he's so used to her being around the clubhouse in the afternoons, it was almost like he was going through withdrawals." Bless her, my bestie lets me get away with my avoidance for the moment.

That gets a genuine laugh from me. I can just imagine that man-child moping around without his fix. He is nothing if not smitten with my employee. "Oh, I wish I could have seen that. Would have been hilarious to watch."

Her responding smile is a little devious. "Yes! All the brothers really gave him a hard time but he didn't let it get to him. He's got it bad for Sarah. I wish she could see that." She looks down at the table like she's said too much.

"What do you mean? I thought she's into him too?" I ask.

All she gives me is a shrug before continuing.

"So, did you miss Ryker as much as you missed me?" The devious little thing, turning the tables on me.

"Ha! Yeah right." *Girl, maybe bring it down a little.*

"How could I miss him when it's my two friends I can't live without?"

"Mmhmm." She's not buying my bullshit either.

"Anyway, you promised me a night at Dean's, remember? I held up my end of the bargain. When are we going?" I have no problem calling in her marker to get that man off the table.

"Does Friday work? Mac wants to go with us. Something about all the men drooling over me the last time we were there." From the roll of her eyes, it's apparent she still doesn't see the beauty the rest of us do.

"Girl. If you were mine, I wouldn't let you walk into that meat market alone either." I say it with a wink just to see her cheeks heat.

Before she gets a chance for a comeback, Sarah calls my name from behind the counter. "Demi! There's someone on the phone for you."

"Okay. I'm coming." I yell back before turning to Kate. "Friday works. I can prep some extra pastries for Saturday morning in case I oversleep. I'll call you later." We stand for a hug before I head back behind the counter to pick up the phone.

"Sweet Treats, this is Demi." I wait for the caller to speak. When there's no response, I try again. "Hello?"

This time, heavy breathing meets my ear. "Hello? How may I help you?"

The weird breathing continues for another ten seconds or so before the call abruptly ends.

Weird. This is so not the town that brings mouth breathers to mind.

Probably just a wrong number. "Hey, Sarah? Did the caller say what they wanted?"

"Just that he wanted to speak to you. Something about your mom?" Sarah answers from where she's multitasking at the counter.

Her words send a shiver down my spine. No one in my life here knows about my mom. Nobody even knows she's the reason I left town.

Before I can let my mind go down that panicked trap, I walk over to where Sarah stands at the counter. "We're going to Dean's on Friday. Do you want to come with?"

She throws me an incredulous look like she can't even fathom that I would want to hang out with her outside of work. "You want me to go with you?"

Yep, my girl doesn't understand that she's been sucked into my orbit.

"Of course. Why would you think I wouldn't?" I ask her.

"Well, um." She stumbles. "I'm sorry. I don't mean to sound rude. It's just that I didn't think you considered me someone you want to hang out with. You know, outside of work."

"Well damn. I must be doing a crappy job at this friend thing with you. Yes, Sarah. I want to hang out with you. You should totally come. We'll have a blast." I tell her.

"Oh, okay. I'll have to see about the kids. With as many hours as I've worked this week, I haven't had as much time with them as I usually do." That's a no if I've ever heard one.

"Alright. I'll give you the out this time but you're definitely not getting out of it next time." I'm still taking those pesky baby steps with her. Unfamiliar territory for a bulldozer like me for sure.

We get back to work, spending the rest of the day working companionably until Joker walks in to pick her up.

"Hey, Demi." He greets me but his eyes devour Sarah at my side. "Wasn't sure if you were back yet. If there's anything you need, Prez said just let us know."

"Thanks, Joker. I'm good." Like I'm going to tell any of the brothers I need help.

That there is the quickest way for my business to get right back to Ryker. I'm not quite ready for more mental warfare with the sexy man.

"Go ahead and head out, Sarah. I've got everything covered here." Really, I am dead on my feet but being away for several days, there are a still some things to catch up on. I'll be here for another few hours before I can even think about heading upstairs.

"Thanks Demi. I'll see you tomorrow morning. Don't work too much longer." She's already pulling on her coat, heading out the door with Joker.

Flipping the sign to Closed, I watch with a smile as they mount Joker's bike and disappear down Main Street. Then I head back to the kitchen.

Music blasting, I spend a productive few hours replenishing my stock of pre-made pastries before I can call it a day.

In the silence, and lack of bustling activity, my thoughts naturally return to my mom, so I grab my phone to text Amy.

Me: Hey how is mom? Any changes?

Amy: Doing good. Fighting doctor's orders to rest and recuperate.

Me: Where do you think I got my stubbornness from? How are you doing?

Amy: Good. I want to come visit you.

This is what I was afraid of when she pestered me with questions about my life here.

Amy is a free spirit like me. Maybe not quite as wild, thank God. I contemplate how to let her down without hurting her feelings when another message comes through.

Amy: Please Demi! I want to see your new home. I miss you!

Way to twist the knife, Sis!

Not sure how to get out of her request, I attempt to put her off for now.

Me: Let me get everything caught up here. It will be a crazy few days until I can get back to a normal schedule again.

Amy: You better! Love you and try not to work too hard!

Me: Love you too! Give mom a hug for me.

As I pour a glass of wine, I contemplate Amy's request and how much risk there could really be in her visiting.

In her defense, nothing unsavory happened while I was in California. No notes, no messages, no cars driving by.

The weird phone call earlier today comes to mind but there is no way Dwight could have found me that fast. No evidence he's even looking for me.

At this point, it's been so long since I left him, he probably doesn't even remember my name. Deciding to sleep on it, I head to bed. I'm way too tired to make a sound decision on so little sleep.

My bed feels heavenly when I collapse on my pillow after taking a quick shower. Even though I'm looking forward to my night out with Kate, I'll need as much rest as possible to shore up my defenses.

Where Mac goes, Ryker is sure to follow. Those men travel as a pack.

I just can't decide if it's apprehension or anticipation coursing through me at the thought of another run in with him.

Chapter Ten

Demi

Friday night finds me once again searching my closet for the perfect outfit to leave the men drooling. Well, more so one guy in particular, but if anyone asks, I'll deny the shit out of it.

A little black dress hiding behind all my other clothes is perfect for tonight's little excursion to Dean's.

The stretchy material hugs my generous curves from breasts to ass and I decide to pair it with my spiked heel boots. The black leather stretches above my knees, leaving several inches of exposed skin below the hem of my dress where it hits mid-thigh.

One last check in the mirror confirms I look good enough to leave all the men panting.

Damn girl. You look good!

Out of excuses to delay, I lock my door and carefully navigate down the stairs for the short walk to Dean's.

The noise of the crowd. The music pumping through the speakers. It all invigorates me as soon as I enter the bar.

The stress of the last several weeks washes away as the beat thrums its way through me. My hips swivel in an instinctual movement as I make my way through the dancing bodies, sidling up to the bar where I find Dean at his usual place serving his customers.

We've developed a friendship of sorts since meeting in this very same spot months ago. He's as big a flirt as me so we get along great.

The volley of come-ons we throw at each other, never taken seriously, has become a game of one-upmanship in our competitive friendship. Since his move back to Frostown a few years back he's created an enticing spot for the locals to hang out.

"Hey Dean! Business is looking good but not as good as you." I throw down the gauntlet when I push my way to the wood topped bar.

"Demi. Dress looks good but it would look even better on my bedroom floor." I snort out a laugh at his comeback. "What's your flavor tonight?"

"Hmm, I think it's a tequila kinda night for me." Might as well get started while I wait for my bestie. Even though it's probably not a great idea to knowingly dull my wits when it's almost a hundred percent sure thing Ryker will make an appearance.

"Living dangerously. I like it. Be right back." He turns to the display of liquor bottles behind him, reaching right for my preferred brand of liquid refreshment.

I snatch up the glass as soon as he sets it in front of me before turning to survey the crowded room as I sip on my shot.

The dance floor is packed, bodies pressed together as people move to the pounding beat. Some in sync. Some not so much. But hey, to each their own, right?

A glance to the game area shows a few men playing a competitive game of pool, while several more look to be locked in an intense round of darts in the corner.

None of the men hold my attention so I swing my gaze back to the main room just in time to catch Ryker striding through the door. My attention immediately captured by the hottie standing a head taller than all those around him.

The power he emanates, without even trying, never fails to send my girly parts fluttering. His self-confidence is undeniably a huge turn on. The fact that he is secure in who he is and is absolutely comfortable with all that control.

The thought of him exerting that power over me as he buries his cock in my pussy is a fantasy that has haunted me since the first time I laid eyes on him in this very establishment.

In this unguarded moment, I soak him in, in all his muscled hotness. It's not often I have the opportunity to observe him without his knowledge and I'm sure as heck going to take advantage as he turns to laugh at something Mac says to him.

The unrestrained joy, the bright smile, is another rarity with this serious man. Understandable with all the responsibility resting on his broad shoulders, running the club and ensuring all the members are safe.

He must feel my eyes on him because his gaze suddenly swings right to me, catching me mid-ogle. Our eyes remain connected for charged seconds before his take a leisurely rove down my body.

That look right there lights me on fire. My body whipped into an inferno in two point five seconds.

I continue to watch unashamedly as he says something to Mac before bee-lining right to where I lean on the bar.

He moves with the grace of a predator stalking its prey. The muscles under his tight black T-shirt flex as he maneuvers through the crowd.

His pace never slows. All too soon he stands right in front of me, his hands gripping the bar on either side of me. His momentum continues until his face rests next to mine. A breath expelled over the shell of my ear causes an involuntary clench in my core. Muscles *quiver*.

Whatever switch he's flipped has increased the temperature to a thousand degrees.

My body is on fire.

Oh girl. You are in so much trouble tonight.

"Demi." His greeting is nothing more than a growl in my ear, just loud enough to be heard over the pounding music.

Just that one gruff word reverberates through my entire body. Shivers break out. My mind blanks as I breathe him in.

I'm not sure what to think of him making a move. He's usually the one keeping distance between us when I get too close. This aggressiveness is new but I have to admit it's potent as hell. Yet a little unsettling after our last conversation.

And I have no idea what to do about it.

"Ryker." Look at me sounding like a phone sex operator.

"Dance with me." It's not a request.

I'm more than a little distracted by the rumble of his voice paired with that growl vibrating through my breasts where we're pressed chest to chest.

He *hovers* over me. A man on a mission.

Words are impossible. Barely can I form a coherent thought in the face of his single-minded focus.

Instead, I pull back just far enough to meet his gaze head on, piercing emerald clashing with striking sapphire.

A silent battle wages, my gaze searching his dominant one for an answer to the questions swirling through my mind.

Recognizing the merit in retreating from this battle, I agree with a single nod.

He gives me no time to second guess my decision, pulling further away to link our hands. Fingers entwined, he drags me away from the bar and hustles me to the dance floor.

The bodies seem to have multiplied in the time since Ryker entered the bar, leaving barely enough space to slip in with the throng of people.

That doesn't deter Ryker, the fact that people scramble out of the way of this intense man probably helps too. He muscles his way to the middle of the dance floor, making room for the two of us.

If you want to call it room.

Hand still gripping mine, he uses his hold to drag my body right up into his personal space. My arms naturally lift to wind around his neck as he slips his around my waist to pull me impossibly closer.

Our bodies move in sync to the beat of the music, lost in the hypnotic bass. I lose track of time. Lost in the feel of his muscles fit perfectly to my soft curves.

Impulsively, I turn my back to him, ass settling firmly in the cradle of his hips. My moves turn sensual, more appropriate for the bedroom than the middle of a packed dance floor.

Ask me if I care in this moment.

I have no control over the sway of my hips as his hard cock rubs erotically against my ass. My arms lift as I lean back to grasp the back of his neck, thankful for the height of my heels. His hands wrap around my hips, fingers rhythmically squeezing, massaging the flesh and pulling me even closer.

I lean back until my head rests on his shoulder, chancing a look up at him.

I find his eyes already on me, desire burning in the endless pools of green. I'm trapped in this moment. Hypnotized. My body swaying perfectly in sync with his.

"Demi!" Our spell is broken when Kate's voice sounds over the pounding music.

From the tone of it, she just might have been trying for a while.

Reluctant to tear my eyes from the intensity that is all Ryker, it takes a great deal of effort to turn my head to find my friend.

When I finally do, I see not only Kate and Mac but Rocker, Bomber and all the ladies from the club dancing around us.

"Hey girl." I greet my friend. "I didn't see you there."

From the conspiratorial smile she shoots my way, she knows exactly who captured my attention but she is way too nice to call me on it. "You want to get a drink with us?"

I'm torn.

A huge part of me doesn't want to leave the perfection of the man at my back but a small sliver of sanity reminds me there is a reason I've avoided him all these months.

The fact that he's switched tactics, added another layer to his game. No longer hiding his desire for me. I still have no idea what to make of it.

It's definitely in my best interest to put some distance between us if I have any hope to survive his onslaught.

That thought right there prompts me to nod. To step away and put that distance between Ryker and me. Following the group to the bar, I find my favorite spot and call out to Dean. "Shots!"

In his usual take charge, 'I'm the boss' kind of way, Ryker muscles up to the bar next to me, propelling the guy on the barstool to my right out of his way. Then, oh my word, he presses all those hard muscles close, caging me in.

The feel of his hard muscles curled protectively around my curves, even through the layers of our clothes, is enough to reignite my desire.

The sexy man isn't giving me any space to shore up my defenses.

The shots Dean places on the bar are a welcome distraction. I snatch up two glasses to hand to Kate and Mac before reaching for another for myself.

Watching those two all lovey-dovey is enough to make me want to puke.

Not really.

I am so happy for my bestie, but the PDA is a bit nauseating. But really only because I'm jealous.

Then again, I only have myself to blame for my lack of a love life. All thanks to my inability to make good decisions about men. At this point, I'm not sure I can trust my own judgement.

Putting those self-deprecating thoughts aside, I turn to the happy couple and raise my glass in a toast. "Congrats! I'm so happy for you guys!"

The beaming smile on Kate's face is overwhelmed by the masculine pride reflected on Mac's as he pulls her close with his arm wrapped around her shoulders.

She fits perfectly to his side, gazing up at him with a soft smile reserved just for him. With the two lovebirds otherwise occupied, I turn to the rest of the group, glass still hanging in the air before throwing the shot back.

"Damn, girl. You better slow down. Last time you celebrated their engagement, Ryker had to carry you out of the clubhouse." Jade shouts over the pounding music.

My surprised gaze flies to the man standing so close, his piercing emerald eyes burning into me. "You took me home that night?"

"Of course. How did you think you got home?" The sexy smirk accompanying his gruff question lifts one side of his mouth.

Damn. I don't think I can handle much more hotness.

"Like Prez was gonna let anyone else take you home drunk off your ass." Mac tears his attention away from my bestie long enough to throw his two cents in the conversation.

Kate rewards his asinine commentary with an elbow to the ribs. "Damn, Siren. What was that for?"

"I think you're spending too much time with Joker." She tells him with a glare. An adorable glare because let's be real, if there is one thing my bestie is not, it's intimidating.

I jump in before the night takes a bad turn for the happy couple. "No worries, Kate. I'm well aware I had a few too many shots that night." I say with a shrug. "It's not every day you get to celebrate your bestie's engagement."

My words have the desired effect. The soft smile that replaces her frown is more her speed. So much more fitting to my bestie's caring personality.

"Nice save, Firecracker." Ryker whispers low enough for my ears only.

Not deigning to give him the satisfaction that his plan is working, I ignore him to wave Dean over, asking for a glass of water.

No need for a repeat of my last night out with the gang. After guzzling down half the glass, I turn the conversation to the other woman quickly becoming a good friend. "I wish Sarah had been able to come tonight. If there's one person that deserves a break, it's her."

"Definitely. She was bummed she couldn't make it out tonight." Kate says.

"We'll have to give her more time to plan next time so she doesn't have an excuse." I really want her to feel comfortable with us and not just when she's working at the bakery.

Ryker takes that moment to remind me he's standing right next to me when he slips his arm along the bar at my back. His fingers slide softly across the fabric of my dress, singeing my skin through the thin material.

When my eyes snap up to his, it's to find his own searing gaze *still* on me. The intensity of his stare fanning the flames of my desire.

And that is how the rest of my night goes. Sharing drinks with close friends, desire simmering just below the surface from the attention of the sexy man that never leaves my side.

I feel safe. Secure in the knowledge that Ryker won't let anything happen to me if I let go.

Before I know it, my bestie is hugging me goodbye before exiting the bar, leaving me alone with the man that takes up way too much of my headspace.

"I'll walk you home." It's not a question. Even though it is literally twenty steps to my apartment, there is no way he'll let me take them on my own.

As we climb the stairs to my apartment, the silence is palpable. The heat of his stare incendiary. When we reach my door, I turn to face him, intent on a friendly goodnight.

The desire in his eyes scatters all intentions of being good.

Before I can second guess myself, I close the distance between our bodies, no more able to control the gravitational pull to this man as the air I breathe.

This magnetism is something I have never felt with another person.

I'm not sure which one of us closes the final distance. Honestly, I don't really care.

All I care about is the touch of his lips on mine as he meets me halfway. Electricity zings as his mouth feathers over mine for the very first time.

He tilts his head, slanting his lips, torturing me in the best possible way. My skin is electrified. All my senses engaged.

Long torturous minutes later, his tongue sensually comes out to play, licking along the seam of my lips, tempting them to part.

I open without hesitation, giving in to his silent command. He takes full advantage as his tongue licks languorously inside my mouth, exploring every recess.

He teases me as our tongues tangle, withholding the pressure I crave. My tongue chases his, not afraid to demand what I want.

He pulls back just far enough to rest his forehead to mine. "Demi." His voice is nothing more than a warning growl as he stares down at me.

"I want you, Ryker." I breathe.

"Do you really?" The deep rasp of his question sets my core on fire. "Or do you just want to be fucked?"

Surprise flickers through me, followed quickly by annoyance. "Does it really matter?"

"Yeah. It matters to me." He gently tucks a wayward strand of hair behind my ear, the tips of his fingers coasting tenderly down my cheek. "I don't think you're ready for what I want."

Sexual frustration combined with the drinks earlier in the night gives way for my uncertainty to slip out. "I'm nothing special, Ryker. Why would you want that?"

His eyes soften, recognizing my insecurity. He cups my cheek with the same reverence he touched my hair.

"Demi, you are special." His eyes hold me captive as he continues. "Everyone makes mistakes. It's the actions that follow that show a person's true character. You may have turned up in Frostown because of a bad decision, but the life you've made for yourself here? It shows me the strong character inside here." His palm settles on my chest, resting right over my heart.

With one more quick press of his lips to mine, he takes my keys to open the door before pushing me over the threshold. "Sweet dreams, Demi."

It's not until I close and lock the door that I hear the echo of his footsteps descending the steps as I press my back to the hard wood.

Chapter Eleven

Ryker

My ride back to the clubhouse is infused with a sense of satisfaction, a high I haven't felt in years. The night just could not have gone any better.

When I first laid eyes on Demi tonight, that scrap of black material covering only the essentials, her tits and ass perfectly outlined?

The beast inside stood up and took notice, ready to drag her out of there to act out every filthy fantasy I've had since I met her.

And I wasn't alone in my greed, all the assholes in the place watched her. The ultimate fantasy, eliciting imaginings of the perfect little body hidden by that little black dress. From the looks on their faces, the same thoughts ran through the mind of every single motherfucker in the place.

It wasn't even a conscious decision to cross the room. I was drawn like a moth to a flame, a dog returning to its master as I stalked her. She was as affected as me, her chest collapsing and expanding rapidly. Breath forcefully moving in and out, pulse racing when I caged her against the bar.

Her easy acceptance when I offered my hand, the vulnerability shone through as her soft palm slipped into mine.

She wanted me. Her need a match to my own.

After months of games, the slightest crack is forming in Demi's tough exterior, allowing the briefest of glimpses to the heart she protects so fiercely.

Color me surprised to find Joker in the main room when I enter the clubhouse. Although not at all surprised to see him alone. He's got it so bad for a certain single mother, there may as well be a neon sign flashing above his head. Sarah's name in big bold letters.

Lost in thought, the thunderous expression is a sure sign he's ruminating on the situation with Sarah's ex. More specifically, the lack of progress in locating him, the elusiveness with which he's evaded our efforts. To say he's pissed is an understatement. Murderous is more like it.

"What's up, brother?" I take the seat next to him.

"Nothin' Prez." He doesn't even look at me.

I weigh the pros and cons of calling him out, ultimately going with my gut. "Sure seems like something is bothering you, Joker."

"Just talked to Byte. Still no update on that motherfucker DeLuca." He grits out, knuckles white from the clench of his fists.

Yep, no surprise this is what's bothering him.

"We'll find him, brother. If there's anyone that can do it, it's Byte. Ya gotta be patient man." I tell him.

"Yeah, yeah. Easy for you to say. You're not the one watchin' what Sarah goes through. Constantly looking over her shoulder. Worried about that asshole showing up to hurt her again." The bang of his fist on the bar booms through the room.

"You think I don't see the same thing as you? I do. You know what else I see?" I don't wait for him to answer. "I see my brother, one of the best men I know, protecting her and her kids. Doing everything in your power to make them feel safe. Cared for. Protected."

But Joker isn't ready to hear it. Instead, he sits there staring mutinously into his beer.

I'm not so sure if he's gonna drink it or throw it.

"Brother don't do anything stupid. Let the club handle DeLuca. Every person in this club, man and woman, will do whatever it takes to deal with him. Trust us to do this for you. For Sarah.

"She needs you. Those kids need you. That should be your focus." I say.

The straightening of his spine is the only sign that he heard a damn thing I said.

Guess that'll have to do for now.

"Think about it. And brother, don't do anything stupid." My work here done, I rise from my stool. My bed is calling my name. The one at home, not at the clubhouse.

"I'm out, brother." I slap him on the shoulder before making my way outside. I take the long way home, my thoughts inevitably returning to the stubborn woman who keeps me awake at night.

It's no secret she's hiding *something*. Secrets from her past she's ashamed of.

The million-dollar question is, is that something still an issue? I intend to get the answer from the woman herself.

Dropping my keys on the kitchen counter, I grab a beer from the fridge and head out to my favorite part of the house, the matching Adirondack chairs on the back of my wraparound porch.

A big part of the reason I chose this town was the natural beauty of the surrounding mountains. The lake surrounded by all that nature called to me on a primal level the first time I ventured out here.

As soon as we voted on our new location, my search began for the perfect spot to build my dream house, my heart set on a lakeside location.

A place to escape from the weight of my responsibilities. Somewhere to go when I need a breather, need to let the mask slip for just a little while.

Settling back in my chair, the stars sparkling off the lake in front of me, I can't help but imagine how much better this would be with Demi relaxing in the seat at my side.

I'll get her there eventually. Just gotta have a little faith.

If I thought I was patient before, that is nothing compared to what's to come.

What she did tonight? Kissing me like that.

Savoring our connection.

Like it was her last first kiss.

She lit my world on fire with just one touch of her lips to mine. I can't even imagine the fireworks when we finally come together but I'm definitely looking forward to it.

All my patience will pay off. Will all be worth it in the end.

She is worth that and so much more.

Whether she knows it or not, she just gave me the opening I was waiting for.

The green light to up my game.

She may not know it yet but I can guarantee she will soon. Damn soon.

With that kiss tonight, she may well have just declared she's mine.

Chapter Twelve

Demi

Back at it in the kitchen early the next morning, I am utterly alone with my thoughts as the sun rises outside the windows. My thoughts and feelings on a never-ending spin cycle since I left Ryker on my doorstep the night before. Sadly, Ryker isn't the only one responsible for my sleepless night. Amy has been harassing me non-stop since I haven't committed to her visiting me. Blowing up my phone, all hours of the day, begging to come see me.

It's not that I don't want to see my sister. I do. I love her to death, and God how I miss her. But is it really safe for her to come here? I could never forgive myself if something happened to her.

Thankfully, I have at least an hour or two before the west coast wakes up. That should give me some time to figure out what to do.

The shatter of glass from the front of the bakery yanks me from my dilemma. No thought to the consequences, I drop the unfinished dough on the counter and beeline straight through the door to the front. Utterly shell-shocked at what I find.

Pieces of glass litter the floor from the shattered picture window of my store front. A faded red brick sits smack dab in the middle of the carnage.

One word.

Bold black letters.

WHORE.

A taunt from an unknown assailant intended to create fear.

But I won't give in. Won't give them the satisfaction.

I am mad.

Angry.

Pissed beyond belief.

Stomping to the kitchen, I grab the broom and dustpan and return to the front. The dustpan bounces off the floor from the force of my frustration. A symphony of scratches from the broken glass under the bristles of my broom screeches through the room as I sweep the shit out of this mess.

I could power a locomotive with the full head of steam building with each swipe across the floor. The curses falling from my lips would earn me a mouth full of soap if my mom could hear me now.

So caught up in my mad, I miss the sound of the front door opening, pausing my rant only when I hear the crunch of glass underfoot. The gasp falling from Sarah's lips.

"Demi! What happened? Are you okay?" She asks with a nervous wring of her hands, anxiety rolling off her in waves.

"Sarah. I didn't hear you come in." I say with a swipe across my brow, my forearm covered in sweat from the force of my cleaning.

"What happened?" She asks again.

"Someone threw a brick through the window." I state the obvious. "Probably just some kids playing a prank."

"A prank? Calling you a whore?" Disbelief colors her voice.

Yeah, girl, I'm not buying it either.

But I've become so good at the lies.

At deceiving my friends.

"Yep." Another one just rolls past my lips.

As I bend down to pick up the brick, Sarah wraps her hand around my wrist.

"Demi, don't. You're going to cut yourself. Go get some gloves first."

She's right. I don't know why I didn't think of that.

"Okay. Be right back. Don't touch anything." I tell her as I hustle back to the kitchen.

Sarah's voice carries through the room when I return to the front, her whispered words cut off as soon as she sees me.

"Who was that?" I ask her.

"No one." My girl refuses to make eye contact.

'Sarah."

Her eyes bob and weave, avoiding eye contact like she's dodging a straight right hook. She could give Jon Jones a run for his money.

What? So mixed martial arts is my guilty pleasure.

Don't knock it til you try it.

All those sweaty men in those short shorts? Sign me up please.

But I digress.

"Who were you talking to?" I press while moving closer.

"Joker." Shoulders slumping, she folds like a house of cards.

Curses fall from my lips.

Dammit. There is no way to hide this from Ryker now.

The sound of pipes roar outside the bakery, so loud I worry the surviving windows will fall too.

They must have been close. There is no way they made time like that from the clubhouse.

Sarah has the good sense to shrink away from the death glare I throw her way as the men dismount their rides.

Ryker is the first man through the door, walking in like he owns the place.

No surprise there.

A pang of longing hits me like a battering ram, smack dab in the center of my chest. Knocks the wind right out of my sails.

But stubborn ass that I am, I refuse to show it.

Like the predator he is, he sees my weakness. Takes a step, then two.

The sexy man stalks me around the bakery like a naughty child escaping a spanking. Words are unnecessary, his intent is clear. Those gorgeous emerald eyes a blazing inferno. He's a powder keg ready to explode.

When did my feet start moving?

He catches me against the counter, caging me in, his knuckles white where he grips the solid wood.

Seems I've provoked the biker and I haven't said a damn word. Even knowing he'll never hurt me, the surge of adrenaline his position invokes is uncontrollable.

His tightly controlled leash is about to snap.

The need to give him a little push, see how quickly he blows, blooms inside me.

"What's wrong, Big Guy? You feeling a little out of control?" I taunt.

He stares me down.

One of his hands slips into the hair at the back of my head. Still no words spoken as his fingers thread up, twisting their way into the hair coiled at the top of my head.

Like a magician, my once tight bun releases, hair cascading over my shoulders where he leans down to bury his face in my tresses. His entire body shudders on a deep exhale.

"So sweet." He murmurs into the curve of my neck. Shivers of excitement explode along the path his lips take, trailing over the sensitive skin to the place where my shoulder meets my neck.

"It's my pastries." I poke the bear.

A huff of laughter is my reward. My triumph at breaking through his serious exterior goes up in flames when Ryker turns his head, shifts impossibly closer. Nibbling over my jaw, he keeps coming until his lips hover a hairsbreadth above my own.

My knuckles ache, clamped firmly around the counter at my hips as I fight the urge to pull his face down to mine. To connect our lips.

To bask in the explosive desire he creates.

And my oh my, he doesn't disappoint, hips shifting, his hardness grinds right where I ache the most.

My lips part on a gasp. One he takes full advantage of. His mouth slamming down on mine, his tongue invading.

This isn't a kiss.

It's a *claiming*.

It is nothing like our first kiss.

From the first touch of our lips, I *ache* with the need for more.

Gone is the controlled nice guy. In his place is a predator with bad intentions. He doesn't ease his way in.

No, this is an all-consuming – take no prisoners – *devouring* of my senses with sharp nips and outright bites of my lips. The abrasion of his stubble just this side of pleasure with a side of pain for good measure.

Sound fades to garbled static in my ears. Fireworks explode behind my eyelids.

I forget I am at work. Forget anyone else is around. Like me, they're all spectators to the ownership this man stamps on me. Right here. Right now.

The air is filled with the sound of raw need as he devours me.

"Oh wow." The awe in Sarah's voice puts a dent the sexual fog Ryker weaves around me.

"Hey Prez. We got a problem here." The seriousness of Joker's words brings me crashing back to reality.

A charged minute ensues as Ryker stares me down. The intensity in those emerald orbs a promise to continue where we left off ASAP.

"What is it?" He releases my gaze, turning to face Joker. If my eyes weren't still stuck on him. If I wasn't watching him so closely, I would have missed the clench of his jaw, the deadly mask slipping over that gorgeous face.

Curious as to the reason for the change, I tear my eyes from this stunning man, casting a questioning look Joker's way.

Then I wished I hadn't.

The words on that brick. What was once hidden now chills my blood. There is only one person with the balls, the sadistic nature to send me that message. FOUND U in bold bloody letters.

Those crudely written words. The warning in that message, I know exactly who just turned my world upside-down.

Chapter Thirteen

Ryker

I watch as all the blood drains from Demi's face, fading away as she does her best Casper impersonation.

Whoever shattered her window, sent her that chilling message? She *knows* who it is.

"Demi. Talk to me. Who did this?" She tears her eyes from the blood chilling message, her gaze drawn back to mine.

Her back straightens, that frustrating mask falling into place. I know before she speaks, lies will fall from those luscious lips.

Leaning down to meet her gaze head on, I warn. "Don't lie to me. I know you know who it is."

"I don't know what you mean, Ryker. I have no idea who did this." She denies.

Our gazes war. Pools of blue flames shoot daggers as her fight returns.

"You think you know everything, Big Guy?" She taunts. "Well, you don't. I already told you. I have no idea who did this."

She holds strong to the lie, her denial just begging for a spanking. Her continued evasion tests my control like nothing ever has before. This woman knows precisely how to push my buttons.

"You sure you want to play this game, Firecracker?" I crowd her back to the counter again, giving her one more chance to come clean. To give me her truth.

Her *trust*.

But from the look on her face, I'm getting nowhere and it pisses me off.

Making a split-second decision, I throw orders to Joker without breaking my stare down with the woman who drives me out of my mind. "Joker, get on the phone. Call the boys over here to board up that window then order a new one. I want it installed yesterday."

Then, surprising the hell out of the woman in front of me, I sweep her up into my arms, heading to the back of the bakery. I carry her through the back door and up the stairs to her apartment. We need privacy for this come to Jesus that is long overdue.

The symbolism of the moment isn't lost on either of us as I carry her bridal style across the threshold to her apartment. Demi is unusually quiet in my arms, perhaps the gravity of her situation is finally penetrating her stubborn exterior.

I hip check the door, satisfied with the loud bang as it slams closed at my back, giving us the privacy I need. Only then do I release the firecracker in my arms, eagerly anticipating the powder keg about to explode.

She doesn't disappoint. Exploding from my arms as soon as her feet touch the ground, a tornado of blond hair swirling around us as she whips to face me.

"What the hell do you think you're doing?" She rants. "How many times have I told you not to manhandle me like that?"

She's beautiful in her anger. Cheeks flushed. Breasts heaving. An irate angel surrounded by a halo of spun gold as her hair settles around her.

This is what I want. This is what draws me in so irresistibly time and time again.

This woman isn't afraid of me. Isn't afraid to stand up to me.

She gives as good as she gets. And she's about to get more than she bargained for.

"Pack your shit. You're coming home with me." The command slips past my lips. The rightness of the words settling like a light in my soul.

"You're out of your damn mind, Ryker. Get out!" I let a smirk slip free, just to see how far I can push her. "Did you hear me? I said get out." Her voice is raising the rafters now.

"The whole damn town heard you, Firecracker." I taunt. "Doesn't change the fact you're coming home with me."

"You are such a controlling bastard!" Chest heaving from the force of her anger, she's never looked more beautiful.

"You may not care about yourself but what about Sarah? What about Kate? What if something happens to them if you put yourself in danger?" I'm a bastard for doing it, but if guilting her into going home with me is the only way to keep her safe? You bet your ass I'll do it.

I will do whatever it takes to keep this woman safe. *Alive.*

"Now you're playing dirty. You know I don't want anything to happen to them." Her shoulders deflate as she huffs her way over to her sofa.

But she wouldn't be the woman who captivates me if she didn't keep up the façade of her displeasure. Throwing the hissiest of all fits, her body drops on the cushions so hard she about bounces off the pillows.

Arms crossed, those breasts prop up like an offering too tempting to refuse. If I had more time here, you can bet your ass we wouldn't be leaving this apartment without a healthy dose of discipline.

"Baby, I'll play as dirty as you want as long as you come home with me." My promise is dark. Provoking images of hot, sweaty, tangled limbs.

With herculean effort, I drag my mind out of the gutter and my eyes back up to hers.

The seriousness of her situation returning.

"I won't let anything happen to you, Firecracker." I promise her. "You can come home as soon as we figure out what's goin' on but you gotta trust me to handle this."

"Fine, Big Guy. We'll do this your way. For now." She stands from the sofa, turning her back on me, leaving me salivating as I watch the hypnotic sway of her ass as she heads to her bedroom to pack.

She turns in the doorway, a sexy smirk on her face when she catches me admiring the view. With absolutely no shame, I adjust my hard cock, letting her take her own fill.

Chapter Fourteen

Ryker

The ride to my house is quiet. A comforting silence as my SUV rolls smoothly down the twisting country roads.

Glancing over, I take advantage of Demi's fascination with the passing greenery to study her in this unguarded moment.

The angle of the sun wraps around her, a halo effect that takes my breath away. The golden rays highlight the tan flesh of her toned thighs, exposed by the cutoff shorts she wears.

A testament to the fact that she's not all work and no play this summer. Most likely Kate's influence, payback for all the times Demi pushed her to stop and be present in the moment.

The urge to touch her, to run my fingers over her flesh, to feel her silky-smooth skin overwhelms me. So much so, I don't fight it. Instead, I give in, reaching over, the skin beneath my hand warm to the touch.

"What are you thinking about so hard over there?" I ask as I trail the tips of my fingers back and forth over all that sleek flesh.

She shivers. As affected by our connection as I am.

"Do you ever wonder what life would be like if you made different choices?" Her words are a whisper, as if she is afraid to tempt destiny.

"Can't say that I have. Every decision I've made has led me to here. Now. With you. I wouldn't change that for anything." Honesty is paramount with this woman. If I want her to let me in, I have to be willing to do the same.

"I don't know what to do about you, Ryker. You're like a mirage. Too good to be true. How am I supposed to trust that it's real?" She huffs out an ironic laugh.

I ruminate on her words. Consider how to respond to keep her from running for the hills. At a loss, and ultimately running out of time when I make the final turn and my house comes into view, I don't respond.

A gasp escapes her, forcefully expelled from her lungs at the sight before us, our conversation momentarily forgotten.

I consider my home through a critical lens, curious what she thinks when she lays eyes on it this first time.

Does she see what I see? The beauty in the solitude?

The rustic two story house, reminiscent of simpler times, sits center stage in a clearing surrounded by nature. The glass surface of the lake glistens in the background, visible just beyond the wraparound porch as I pull the SUV into the garage.

I jump out, rounding the front bumper to open Demi's door for her before reaching into the backseat to grab her bag. She packed light, probably expecting a quick return to her home above the bakery.

Little does she know, now that I have her in my space, I'll use every trick in the book to entice her to stay.

That plan starts with gaining her trust, breaking through her walls. Getting to her secrets.

I've respected her privacy, her need for space with the hope she'll come to me in her own time. Share her secrets when she was ready.

I see the error of my ways now. A bulldozer like Demi, what she needs is a strong hand, needs to see that she can't scare me away. Nothing in her past will change the way I feel about her.

Only then, when she truly believes in me. In *us.* Only then will she trust me enough to give me her truth. Her secrets.

I follow her as she moves through the house, matching her step for step as she takes in my home. I keep her in my sight, anxious to catch her reaction.

After several quiet moments, I urge her on.

"Come on. I'll show you to your room." I lead her up the staircase, down the hall to the room next to mine. She may not be with me yet but that doesn't mean I can't keep her close.

"That's my room." I point out the closed double doors. "You need anything at all, you come find me."

I set her bag on the guest room bed and turn to give her some privacy.

Stopping in the doorway, I lean a shoulder against the wood frame when I catch her eyeing me, letting her look her fill.

"I'll be out on the back deck if you're interested in joining me." I offer.

It's the hardest thing to do, walking away, hoping beyond hope she takes me up on the offer.

Fifteen minutes later my patience is rewarded. Nursing a whiskey, I catch sight of her floating down the stairs and out the patio doors. Those teasing cutoff shorts should be illegal, flashing me just a glimpse of that spankable ass before she drops down next to me.

"Wow. This is beautiful." Her words distract me from my illicit fantasies. So many fantasies – too damn many to name. I could go on for days.

"Yeah. It's why I bought the property." I admit.

"I can see why. There's a peace here you don't get in town. Even in a town as small as this one." She says.

Her words calm the nerves I didn't even realize were buzzing through me since I brought her into my home. They reinforce my decision to bring her here, to share this with her.

And the sight of her sitting there, in the chair next to mine, just like I imagined? God, was it just last night? The band tightening my chest snaps, the rightness of this moment burrowing deep down into my soul.

The need to make this permanent – to have her here every night – is fiercer than ever. Lights a fire in my blood. I'll do whatever it takes to make it happen.

I'm bowled over by the sereneness on her face. A calmness I've never seen that downright changes her entire demeanor. Gone is the ballbuster. In her place is the woman I have only caught glimpses of in the past. But is exactly the one I want by my side.

She is a beautiful sight to see in this moment. The setting sun glistening off the surface of the lake casts an ethereal glow around her. Her golden locks a halo in the fading light.

We sit in silence, savoring the moment, as the last rays of light fade into the night, the stars dancing across the lake in a synchronized swim.

Chapter Fifteen

Demi

Sunlight streams through the picture window in Ryker's guest bedroom, waking me from a dead sleep the next morning. Probably the best sleep I've had since my hasty escape from California.

There is only one thing that could make this better – waking up all wrapped up with Ryker instead of alone in this luxurious bed. Although that option comes with more strings than I think I'm ready for.

Bits and pieces of the previous evening flutter in, playing like a movie reel in my head.

The beauty of Ryker's home.

The soft lap of the lake rolling in along the shoreline. A wave of calm washed over me as soon as I walked out his patio doors.

The quiet.

The peace in the calm of my surroundings. Such a surprise for someone constantly going a mile a minute.

Hell, who am I kidding? It was all emanating from the man sitting right there in front of me. Everything about this strong, stoic man brings me a sense of peace that has been sadly lacking in my life.

So, I let him reel me in, a need so strong I didn't even fight it. My feet carried me to the chair at his side without direction from my brain.

The moment was perfect. Peaceful.

That peace lulled me into a sense of security, so much so, I nodded off in my chair. And then the faintest recollection of Ryker's arms cradling me close. The softest whisper of his lips brushing over my forehead as he laid me on the guestroom bed like I was made of spun glass.

I felt cherished.

Cared for.

Taken care of.

Secure.

And let me tell you, that is a feeling that has definitely been lacking in any of my previous relationships.

Isn't that a depressing thought?

Deciding not to dwell on that, I climb almost regretfully from the luxurious cloud and head to the bathroom across the hall.

After brushing my teeth and washing my face, I set out to explore Ryker's home in the light of day.

As I wander, I realize the fading sunset did not do this house justice last night. Ryker has created an enticing oasis that I never want to leave.

So not what I was expecting from the serious man that runs his club with an iron fist. Every room I look into is more homey than the last.

His living room showcases not an ultra-modern black leather couch but rather a tan sectional with cushions so soft it brings to mind cold rainy days snuggled up next to Ryker. Hogging the blankets. Stealing his body heat.

"Mornin'." That deliciously rough word scrapes down my spine like a lover's caress as if conjured from my daydream.

I turn, ready to return the greeting, but the words get stuck in my throat. My mouth goes as dry as the Sahara. All for the shirtless hottie leaning against the wall across from me. Arms crossed, those beautiful muscles look carved from marble.

My mind goes stupid. I'm a statue that can do nothing but gawk.

Eyes don't blink.

Words won't come.

But oh, do I look. My eyes roam over his face, short, neat beard that highlights that granite jaw. Broad shoulders I know from experience can hold my curvy figure no problem.

Expansive chest, sharp pecs sporting intricately woven tattoos. Over perfectly chiseled abs, his happy trail a treasure map leading down to his tantalizing Adonis belt until sadly it disappears into his sweatpants. The grey material just barely clinging to his hips.

The man is *built*. So freakin' sexy it is impossible to look away. Impossible not to feel inferior with my ass that has seen more than its fair share of my sweet treats.

Never before have I reprimanded myself for a bit of overindulgence when testing my baked concoctions.

Until now.

Until I'm faced with this perfect specimen of a man that looks like he has never been tempted. Would laugh in the face of a frivolous pastry attempting to pass those kissable lips.

My girly parts sure do take notice.

My thighs clench, wetness weeping from my core.

Just a regular occurrence any time I'm around this man.

"Demi?" Ryker's amused voice brings me crashing back to reality.

From the question in his tone, he might have been trying to capture my attention for a minute. Maybe more.

And yep, when I oh so slowly drag my eyes back up to his face, there is a whole lot of humor lining his smile. Like he *knows* what he does to me. The draw he has.

I swallow down the drool pooling in my mouth so I can answer him, barely holding back a swipe across my mouth in case any escaped.

"Good morning." I say.

Don't judge. That's about all I can manage in the face of all his sexiness first thing in the morning.

Now that I take a closer look at his face, it seems he might be suffering from the same debilitation. The inability to stop looking.

My nipples harden, doing their best high beam impersonation behind the thin material of my black tank. A girl can only hope the dark cloth hides the reaction.

Sadly, from the smirk tilting his lips with a glance down at the girls, he doesn't miss a thing.

"I asked if you want some coffee?" Thankfully, he doesn't comment on my body's affliction.

"Sure." I follow him when he beelines for the coffee maker.

Don't think for a minute I missed the fact that my dream kitchen exists right here in front of me. It took every ounce of willpower I possessed to trap the squeal of my fifteen-year-old self at my first boy band concert when my eyes took in his kick ass kitchen.

Sleek black stainless-steel appliances, highest end outside a Michelin star restaurant, are surrounded by grey and white marbled countertops. The industrial size refrigerator and freezer. The double ovens. An abundance of counter space.

All combined to steal my baker's heart.

I couldn't have done better designing the perfect kitchen myself.

"I have to go to the clubhouse for a couple hours." Ryker pulls me out of my fan girl moment.

"Okay." I say. "What am I supposed to do while you're gone?"

Another smirk lights his face, nowhere near hidden behind the rim of his coffee cup. "The pantry and fridge are fully stocked. I can see you're dying to break in my kitchen."

Well, shoot. How can I resist that temptation? There's only one problem.

"Are you going to be my taste tester if I do?" The taunt flies past my lips without permission. But it's too late to take it back now.

Not sure I want to if the flare of his nostrils, the heat in his gaze is my reward.

He stalks me around the counter, setting his cup down even as he invades my personal space. And he doesn't stop there.

No, he keeps coming until there's not an inch of space separating us, the heat of his chest singeing me down to my toes.

Leaning down, he makes sure he has my full attention before speaking. "Demi. I'll taste whatever you want me to. Any time. Anywhere."

Oh boy. I think my panties just went up in flames.

This Ryker? This version of unleashed sexual intent will be my undoing.

He doesn't wait for me to acknowledge his offer. "Do an inventory. If there's anything you need, text me and I'll have it for you by the time I get back." He says. "But first, savor the morning. Take your coffee out on the back deck. You work too hard."

His command is softened by the brush of his hand over my waist, fingers ghosting over the inch of exposed skin between my tank and sleep shorts. Tingles ignite, awareness skittering over my skin. A craving like never before to feel his touch on other parts of my body.

Sheesh. When he sets his mind to something, Ryker does *not* play around.

"I'm gonna shower." His breath tickles over my neck. His words a whisper of temptation igniting my imagination.

Ryker naked in the shower. Water cascading over his deliciously hard body. Would he put on a show if I snuck in there to watch?

Something tells me he wouldn't accept anything other than full participation on my part.

Pulling away all too soon, he presses a faint kiss to my forehead then backs away. His intelligent eyes miss nothing.

The galloping pulse at the base of my neck, my heaving breasts, my labored breathing. He takes it all in. His predatory gaze unwavering as he backs out of the kitchen, turning at the last second to walk away.

Damn, it is a sin to look just as good from the backside.

This man will be the death of me.

How in the hell am I going to survive living with him?

Chapter Sixteen

Demi

I'm elbow deep in cake batter when the pipes of Ryker's motorcycle roar through the garage. I stand frozen in place, a deer in the headlights, as he saunters into the house. Unsure of myself for the first time in forever. No idea how he'll react to me taking over his kitchen even though he gave me full rein.

From the sight of the bag in his hand, he came through on his promise to pick up the grocery list I sent him.

I *feel* his scrutiny as he stops right inside the kitchen, shoulder leaning against the doorframe. His gaze roves my body, a trail of fire left in its wake. My skin tingles, sparks shoot straight through my belly. My traitorous heart wishing it was his hands, not his eyes, roaming my body instead.

Embarrassingly, I have to clear my throat before speaking. "Hey. Thanks for picking up my stuff."

"No problem." He says but makes no move to come further into the kitchen. *That just won't do.*

In a split-second, I decide to see if I can push him as far out of his comfort zone as I am.

"Would you set them over here?" I tempt him to close the distance between us.

He doesn't disappoint. Crossing the floor, he steps right up behind me, resting his chin on my shoulder to check out the concoction I'm in the middle of.

Cakes and cupcakes aren't my usual thing, but I've been playing around with a new idea. With down time for the foreseeable future, now is the perfect time to do some experimentation. See if this is something I can add to the menu on the regular.

"It'll be a few days before we can get your window replaced. A week at most." Definitely not what I want to hear.

Guess I really do have time to perfect these beauties.

Tension builds as his presence surrounds me, his scent invading my senses. All I want to do is turn around and bury my face in his neck, take a deep inhale of the masculine mix of leather, motor oil and whiskey. The combination shouldn't make sense, but for some reason it works perfectly on Ryker.

Boy, does it work for him.

Heat emanates from his body. Singes my backside where he stands so close behind me even though our only connection is his chin on my shoulder.

This man generates a boatload of sexual energy. I've had sex that was less potent than the feel of him standing so close, fully clothed in his kitchen.

All of it combines for a tease to my senses.

I've had boyfriends, even a one-night stand. But none of those experiences hold a candle to the man at my back. His intensity, the way he towers over me. He overwhelms every single one of my senses. His mere presence inspires feelings I have no experience with.

As much as he turns me on – intrigues me – he scares me just as much. Maybe more. This man has the power to break me. To shatter the carefully constructed life I've created since escaping my past.

After a minute of tense silence, Ryker makes a move, but not the one I expect. He steps back, taking all his deliciousness just out of my reach.

"You want some help?" His question surprises me.

So much so, I swing around too quickly, the spatula in my hand completely forgotten. That is until batter flies through the air, landing on his pristine white T-shirt. A snort of laughter escapes me as he stares down at the offending spot.

That laughter dies a quick death when his intense eyes rise to mine.

"I'm sorry." I start but he's already on the move, a new gleam lighting those emerald orbs. A playfulness he's never shown me before.

He crowds me back against the counter and this time he doesn't keep his distance. No, he keeps right on coming until our fronts press together. *Hard.*

Breath whooshes from my lungs as I fight the urge to rub myself all over him like a cat in heat. Because let's be real, that is exactly how I feel right now. Reduced to my basest instincts, lost in this mating ritual as old as time.

"You're in trouble now." He warns.

My body screams in protest when he moves away as quickly as he advanced. I don't even realize he stole my spatula until more batter flies through the air, the cold gooey mixture landing on my cheek with a plop.

I gape at the man in front of me, smirk tilting one side of his mouth as he raises the spatula to run his tongue along the edge.

I swear I feel that lick right on my clit. My pussy weeps, clenching and releasing, crying out for the same attention from his tongue. The fact he keeps that intense gaze fastened to mine the entire time certainly doesn't help matters.

"Delicious." A deep moan rumbles through me at that one growled word.

As I fight to contain it, he stalks right back in my personal space. A predator on the move, Ryker comes impossibly closer. Bending low, he swipes that devilish tongue across my cheek, cleaning up that spot of batter.

Oh, so slowly.

Who knew Ryker was such a torturous tease.

God knows, stoic and serious Ryker is hot. But this playful version? This man with his guard down? He is sex on a stick.

And I have no idea what to do with him.

Luckily, he makes a move before I have to decide, taking my hips in his strong grip, he hoists me up onto the counter. With a mind of their own, my legs spread automatically to make room for his big body.

He is at the perfect height to feel the proof of his arousal, his hardness notched right where I need him most, pressing the seam of my shorts right on my clit. The pressure just what my body craves.

Leaning in, he ghosts his lips over mine, a decadent mix of chocolate and minty freshness alive on his tongue. Reminiscent of hot summer nights, indulging in my favorite mint chocolate chip ice cream to stave off the heat.

Our tongues tangle. Breath mingles. Arousal spikes as he explores my mouth. Tongue licking and retreating, mimicking the dance I ache for with his cock thrusting deep inside my core.

Moans fall past my lips, caught up in the desire this sexy man invokes like no other. I rub myself against him shamelessly, seeking the pressure I need to detonate.

But Ryker pulls away suddenly, leaving me hanging on the edge of the precipice. My breasts heave. Forceful pants expanding my ribcage as I watch him withdraw helplessly.

"I shouldn't have done that." Regret fills his eyes.

Rage explodes inside me. This man has been playing me like a yo-yo for months. Just when I thought we were on the same page, he pulls this bullshit. Jumping off the counter, I refuse to be embarrassed at what we did.

"Right." I say, not even deigning to acknowledge his regret. "The oven is ready. I'm gonna get back to it."

Confusion lights his eyes. Caution lines his face. Probably expecting me to explode. Throw a fit.

It stings that it is precisely what I would have done in the past but I'm not gonna give him the satisfaction.

Turning back to the mixing bowl, I listen as his footsteps fade down the hallway before the sound of his office door closes.

He can run but he can't hide. If Ryker feels half of what I feel when we get lost in each other, sooner or later, he is going to fold.

And fireworks will explode.

Chapter Seventeen

Ryker

The stillness of my house greets me when I enter through the garage, surprising considering how much life Demi has already infused into the place.

It's been only seven days, but in that time, Demi has put her own unique stamp on my home. More color. More lightness.

And the smells? They are amazing. From her baking to her body wash. There is nowhere for me to escape the allure of Demi living here with me.

It is the sweetest kind of torture.

A week of her scent invading every inch of my home. A week of her parading around in the skimpiest of clothes. Something I damn well know she's doing on purpose to get a rise out of me.

If only she were as free with her emotions as she was with her body. That right there is what's held me back.

Every time I turn around, there she is to test my control. The only place I get any kind of a reprieve is behind the closed doors of my office.

As I wander through the house, double checking the locks on all the doors and windows, I can't help but wonder where she lurks tonight, planning her next sensual assault.

I know she didn't leave. The prospect watching my house reported a quiet night while I was at the clubhouse.

Funny enough, our roles have reversed over the last seven days. What was once my sanctuary has become the place I avoid, my willpower waning in the face of the temptress within.

Maybe she made an early night of it.

That wishful thinking is blown out of the water as I draw closer to my open bedroom door. The faint rasp of sheets, an indrawn breath, alert me to the presence of the woman that haunts my dreams.

What I wasn't prepared for? The sight of her in my bed, head thrown back, sheet draped over her body as a distinctly erotic moan escapes her sinful lips. My gaze is riveted as the sheet falls to her waist, revealing the fact she's already pushed up her tank, the material resting in the vicinity of her collarbone. My hungry eyes eat up the sight of her perfect breasts exposed to me for the first time.

I am a voyeur in my own damn house.

My cock turns to steel when her raised knees spread, falling to the sides under the sheet, the movement of her hands hidden from my view.

My imagination runs wild as her moans echo through the room, control snapping when my name falls from her lips. The tight leash obliterated by that one whispered word.

I move across the room without direction to my feet, stopping a foot from the bed, eyes glued to my wet dream come to life.

Demi's eyes flutter open, the sound of my footsteps alerting her to another presence in the room. Her hands freeze under the sheet and that is downright unacceptable.

"Ryker." She's breathless, so beautiful, lost in the fantasy that drove her to my bed.

"Don't stop." I rasp, daring her to keep going.

Her eyes stay locked to mine. A tense minute passes as our gaze's war until *finally* the sheet starts twitching again.

But that just won't do. If she's going to tempt me, the least she can do is really put on a show. I reach my hand out, slowly dragging the sheet away.

Agonizingly slowly, her gorgeous body is revealed to me for the very first time. She's shed her shorts, removed her panties. All I see is her hand buried in her perfect little pussy.

Fingers glistening, she circles her clit. Back arched, she is thoroughly lost in the fantasy she's created.

"Look how wet you are. Is that all for me, Firecracker?" The question scrapes past my throat, voice raw.

A whimper is her only answer but it's not nearly enough.

"Answer me, Demi. Is this what you wanted when you snuck into my bed like a thief in the night?" I demand, pressing my hand to my cock where it strains to escape the confines of my jeans.

"Yes." She breathes.

"Wanted to push me over the edge? All the cock teasing this week didn't get you what you wanted?" God knows I was tempted.

I have jacked off an embarrassing number of times over the past week. Taken too many cold showers to count. All because of this woman.

"Ryker." If there was any doubt my dominating ways were a turn on for her. The whine escaping her lips, the shake of her thighs even as she drops her knees to the sides, opening herself up to my hungry gaze. All of it confirms this woman wants me just as I am.

"I told you not to stop. Keep teasing your clit." I command.

Following directions beautifully, her fingers start circling her clit once again, a featherlike touch to hold herself just this side of ecstasy.

"Are you imagining it's me? My fingers giving you the pressure you need. Teasing that pretty little pussy until you shatter?" I push, testing her limits as I touch her bent knee, gliding the tips of my fingers along the skin of her silky-smooth thigh.

A loud moan is my reward, urging me onward until I reach the juncture of her trembling thighs. Her hips raise, offering herself to me, to the pleasure I can bring her.

"Ryker." Her stomach quivers, ribs expanding and contracting from the force of her pants.

"You want my fingers inside you, Firecracker?" I've never been this vocal in bed.

Never had this driving need to push my previous partners past the point of no return so spectacularly. But Demi is different. I want to test her. Push her out of her comfort zone. See how high I can make her soar.

With her wetness easing the way, I slip and slide through the lips of her sex until I reach her opening, pausing to tease my fingers in a circle around it. Not giving her the fullness she needs to go over the edge. Her hips lift, chasing the pressure.

Just the reaction I was waiting for.

I take that as my cue to drive two fingers inside her. Precum escapes when her tight pussy spasms, my cock on a mission to fill her to overflowing.

"Come for me, Firecracker." My command is the push she needs. Pussy clenching impossibly tighter, a rush of wetness coats my hand as a silent scream escapes with the power of her orgasm.

I coax her down from her peak, gentling the thrust of my fingers until her body falls limp. Relaxed. Satiated.

Masculine pride wars with my own need to come. Seeing this independent woman, with a backbone of steel, come undone on my command steals the breath from my lungs.

"You good?" I ask her, fingers still teasing her opening.

"Yeah. You?"

A bark of laughter escapes. I can't help it. I am so far from good, strung so tight, it's laughable.

Demi reaches for the clasp of my belt but I settle my hand over hers. "Demi, no."

"Please Ryker. I just want to see you." She begs so prettily, I don't have it in me to say no.

She must see it on my face because her nimble fingers go to work on the button and fly of my jeans.

My cock throbs with want. Want to be inside her. Want to feel her hands on it.

Want.

Want.

Want.

That's all I ever feel with this woman. The need for more is all-consuming.

Her soft hand wraps around my hard length. The perfect pressure shocking me back to the reality of the moment.

Soft touch to hard steel as she strokes me from root to tip.

I pull off my shirt, vision going black for just a second. All I feel is the perfection of her touch. Quickly discarding it, my jeans and boxer briefs go next as I toe off my boots.

Then I am as naked as she is. Standing to my full height, I tower over her petite form where she kneels on the edge of my bed. Wrapping my hand around her wrist, I still her movements.

"Lay back down. Exactly how you were." I tell her, following her down onto the bed when she complies.

She's a vision laid out in front of me. Head resting on my pillow, knees raised, wetness still coating the lips of her pussy, right where my cock aches to be.

I walk forward on my knees, moving right up between her splayed thighs until I'm cushioned under the swell of her ass. The first touch of my sex to hers lights an electric shock down my spine. So strong I jolt from the impact. Thrusting forward and back, I tease her clit with the head of my cock. Short bursts mixed with long strokes. From the glazed look in her eyes, her desire is reigniting, building just as quickly as my own.

What I wouldn't give to drive balls deep. Thrust home to glory in the tight heat of her pussy as it strangles my cock.

I lift a hand to tease her breast, a gentle squeeze to her tip, pushing her to her peak faster.

"Harder." She begs and I happily comply with her demand.

She squirms with the added pressure, seeking to line me up to breach her entrance, but I remain strong. Stay just out of sync.

"Fuck, Demi."

One stroke then two. The second hits her clit just right. On the third stroke we both explode. My come hits her pussy, coating her in my release, aiding my movements even as more shoots up onto her belly.

Marking her.

Mine.

The thought plays on a loop as I collapse on top of her. Breath expels from my lungs. A soft breeze fluttering her hair where I've planted my face in her neck. My heart pounds as I recover from the hottest sexual experience of my life.

This woman does something to me without even trying.

Reluctantly, I pull away. Standing from the bed, I head to the bathroom, grabbing a towel to clean her up. A wave of disappointment washes through me as I wipe away the evidence of my marking.

Demi studies me. Probably trying to figure out how the hell I'm gonna handle the situation when I've clearly avoided just this for the past seven days.

Recognizing a losing battle, I give in to the urge and pull her down next to me. All feels right in my world as I wrap her in my arms.

"Get some sleep." I tell her as I trace the tips of my fingers up and down her spine. She curls into me, a satisfied sigh escaping before her breathing evens out.

As I stare blankly at the ceiling, I contemplate the turn this night took and how the hell I'm going to keep this woman in my life and not just in my bed.

Chapter Eighteen

Demi

The warm rays of sunshine streaming through the window gently wake me from another great night of sleep. This time in Ryker's bed. As I raise my arms, stretching full out, the weight of his arm tightens around my waist.

I fight the urge to settle back into him, to glory in this new sense of comfort that's been severely lacking in my lonely existence.

I may play the part of happy go lucky, but it's all a sham. What I crave more than anything is to have a person I can rely on. My gut tells me that someone is right beside me, holding me so protectively, even in his sleep.

The problem is, my gut steered me so wrong in my last relationship, I'm way too scared to trust it now.

Dwight may have sent me running in fear but Ryker? Ryker has the power to destroy me. And I'm not just talking physically. If I entrust my heart to him, and he lets me down? I really don't think I could survive a betrayal like that.

Somehow, someway, this man is chipping away at my defenses and I am terrified. So terrified to give him what he's been so bluntly clear he wants.

Casual sex will never be enough with this man. No, he wants it all, and for some reason, he sees what he wants in me. A future I'm too afraid to hope for. Let's be real here. I am a straight up coward. Too afraid to fall without the safety of a net.

On that depressing thought, I slip from the bed. Finding Ryker's shirt from the night before, I can't resist slipping the soft material over my head. The alluring scent that is all Ryker wraps me up like a security blanket the same as he did all night.

That's all the reminder my brain needs to take me right back to last night when he caught me getting off in his bed, surrounded by this same intoxicating scent.

I'm not stupid, Ryker has been avoiding me like the plague since giving me just a glimpse of his playful side when he helped me in the kitchen last week. Although, help may not be the right word. More like he fried my brain so bad I had no clue what ingredients to add to the mixer and I created that freakin' recipe.

Knew it by heart.

He is that *potent*.

Slipping out of the room on silent feet, I trek down the stairs and into the kitchen. My brain is in desperate need of a distraction and baking is just the thing to do it.

Without Ryker there to drool over, I should be able to knock out a batch of cinnamon buns. I'm firing on all cylinders but that will change with a quickness as soon as he graces me with his hotness.

With my ingredients on the counter, I get right to work. Folding in the flour, I knead the dough like it did me wrong as I ponder what to do about that man. With a huff, I set it aside so I don't overwork the mixture.

Butter sizzles when I drop it into the searing pan with every intention of refocusing to perfect this recipe.

That lasts two point five seconds.

Before I know it, memories of the night before invade once again. So lost in the fantasy of Ryker catching me in his bed, I didn't hear him until it was too late to realize the fantasy had become a reality.

My cheeks burn as hot as the butter sizzling in the pan when I add sugar and cinnamon.

The crazy notion that I could do what I was doing, and get away with it? I see the error of my ways now.

Although, I sure can't complain about the outcome. We may not have gone all the way but boy oh boy, the intimacy of Ryker commanding my orgasm. Hawk like gaze taking in every detail of the way I played my body, hyper focused on my pleasure.

Is it hot in here? How high did I set the temperature on the oven?

And when he climbed naked on the bed, my thighs snapped open so fast they gave me whiplash. With the head of his cock teasing my clit on every upward thrust, my second orgasm rose like a tsunami, washing away any hesitation, any embarrassment at getting caught red-handed.

He was everything I imagined and so much more.

Commanding.

Hot.

Dominating.

That was, by far, the single hottest sexual encounter of my life. If we light up the sheets without actual penetration, I just know the world will tilt on its axis when we go all the way.

That thought right there. It scares the shit out of me. This man is chipping away at my defenses. Brick by brick, he's getting through to the heart of me. Getting to my truth when I'm not ready to trust my judgement.

The ring of my phone draws me from the memory of the best sex of my life. Probably for the best, I don't have the mental capacity to think about the consequences right now.

I hesitate at the sight of a blocked number. The call at the bakery, the brick through my window, all seeming coincidences combine to freeze my hand as I reach for it.

Before I can decide what to do, Ryker's hand is there, snatching the phone out from under my fingers and takes the decision completely out of my hands. I squeak in surprise when I realize the jerk snuck up on me in the middle of my fantasy.

But I can't dwell on that right now. All seeing eyes take in every emotion that crosses my face as he raises the phone to his ear. "Hello."

Anticipation chokes me while I wait with bated breath and dreadful anticipation of any hint of who is on the other end.

"Who is this? What do you want?" From the tightening of his jaw, it is nothing and no one good.

"Motherfucker, stay the hell away from her." Ryker drops the phone from his ear, making no move to end the call.

His emerald eyes pierce me, feeling a lot like he sees straight down into my soul.

"Who was that?" I'm almost afraid to ask but I need to know.

"You want to explain why some asshole is claiming to be your boyfriend?" He's pissed.

Angrier than I have ever seen him.

But his words make no sense.

"What? I don't have a boyfriend, Ryker." I tell him the truth.

"That's not what *Dwight* said." He spits out.

Chapter Nineteen

Demi

Oh God.

The walls close in around me.

My lungs are frozen. Lips flap but no sound escapes. I am a fish out of water.

Just like that, my carefully constructed house of lies has folded. The lies so good, I fooled even myself.

My God, I am such an idiot.

But not anymore. Now more than ever, I need to get out of here. Need an escape plan now that Dwight has somehow found me.

The anger on Ryker's face is the absolute last thing I can deal with right now. I need to figure a way out of here. A way out of this town. A way to keep the people I care about safe. Starting with this perfect man.

"I have to go." The dough on the counter is forgotten. The warming oven at my back stifling as panic builds inside me. A geyser looking for a crack to explode.

And through it all Ryker watches me. Studies the myriad of emotions I'm sure are racing over my face.

The fear. The panic. The *anguish* at the thought of leaving this sleepy little town. At the thought of leaving *him*.

"Demi." The warning in Ryker's voice goes straight over my head.

I turn to escape the kitchen. Escape this man that sees too much of me.

But he doesn't let me. He wraps an arm around my waist, dragging my back to his front, anchoring me to him like a lifeline.

"Talk to me, Firecracker." The whisper of his voice softens the command in his tone.

Talk? Is he crazy?

How can he not hear the air whooshing in and out of my lungs?

How can I talk when I am incapable of nothing but hyperventilating?

"Breathe, baby." His hand settles on my chest, a heavy weight forcing my lungs to slow. "Come on, Demi. Feel me. Deep breath in. Slow exhale out."

His actions match his words, his chest expanding and caving at my back. A gentle rolling up and down, back and forth, he soothes my nerves like the lap of waves on the lakeside shore.

I follow his lead, matching him breath for breath.

Ryker's other hand gently slides up the sensitive skin of my arm, continuing on until his fingers glide into the hair at the nape of my neck.

"Close your eyes, Demi." His voice is softer, breath whispering over the shell of my ear as those fingers massage away the tension held at the base of my neck.

Ryker's commanding presence overwhelms me, once again stalling the even pattern of my breathing as I hang on his every word.

"Relax." The fingers in my hair tighten, bordering just this side of pain.

"I don't know how you expect me to relax with you doing that." I can't help the sarcasm lacing my words.

Desire pools in my belly as I anxiously anticipate whatever he'll do next.

"Smartass. Close your eyes." The hand on my chest slides down through the valley of my breasts, circling my belly button when he reaches my stomach.

His fingers in my hair tighten, using his hold to turn my face to his.

My pulse spikes for an entirely different reason this time. Gone is my panicky racing heart of two minutes ago.

This is a powerful pounding that sends my heart galloping, blood racing to my breasts, my nipples. Downright electrifying my clit.

"Ryker." I moan out his name as his mouth ghosts over mine.

With my eyes closed, sensation takes over. My skin burns, nerve endings sizzle.

His lips trace back and forth over my own. Not quite a kiss. No, this is a savoring of our connection as he works to calm me down.

When his name escapes my lips for a second time, all bets are off. His leash snaps and his mouth covers mine completely.

Air whooshes from my lungs as he straight up devours me. Tongue licking the deepest recesses of my mouth and just like last night, he demands my full participation.

Suddenly, our positions are reversed, my body plastered to the counter, he presses me down without breaking the connection of our mouths. Hips grinding, the hard length of his arousal fits perfectly against my ass.

Tasting of mint and deliciously hot male, Ryker builds an inferno of bubbling lava in my belly. Gone is my panic, my mind one hundred percent caught up in a sexual awakening.

"God, you feel so good." The words rumbled from his chest are punctuated by a sharp nip of my lip.

I release a gasp in pleasure when he slips his hand inside my panties, no shame at the wetness that only serves to spur him on.

"So wet." He teases my clit, a finger on either side of it. Sliding up and down, the torturous man refuses to give me the firm pressure I need.

"Ryker. Please." I'm not above begging at this point.

"Promise me you won't run, Firecracker." He demands.

All the while, that delicious friction builds, my orgasm nearing the precipice, his words incomprehensible in the heat of the moment.

"I need more." I tell him, hips swiveling, chasing the pleasure only he can give me.

"Promise me, Demi. You need to trust that I will take care of this. Take care of *you*. You don't have to be scared anymore." He promises.

But promises are made to be broken. Ask any one of my previous boyfriends. Not one of them could tell you with a straight face they never broke a promise to me.

He moves his hand down to thrust two fingers inside me, thumb finally moving over my clit, giving me the pressure I need to soar.

"Yes!" I explode. If I could think beyond my orgasm, I might be embarrassed at the screech of my voice.

Slumping over the counter, the cold granite cools my heated skin as Ryker continues to stroke me, soft touches to bring me down gently from the high of my peak.

With his other hand he gently strokes the hair away from my face, forcing me to acknowledge the truth in his words. Eyes intense, he waits for my brain to come back online.

"We're goin' to the clubhouse." His words are a splash of icy water.

They bring me right back around to the panic of Dwight finding me.

"Ryker. I can't. I couldn't live with myself if something happens to you." The words escape unplanned.

I've done so well, keeping him at a distance. All it took was one phone call from my ex, one explosive orgasm, to give him the opening to sneak his way past my defenses.

"Demi. Don't push me away. We can handle this. Nothing is gonna happen to me. You need to let me in." His lips coast over the shell of my ear.

I have no idea how he has the ability to rebuild my desire so quickly but I am right back to the edge once more. It's laughable, the hold this man has over me.

"Just give me this. Please." He says.

Dammit.

It's the pleading that breaks me. This is a man who is *always* in control. For him to let down his guard. To ask instead of demand. I have no hope of denying him his request.

"Okay."

God help me if anything happens to the ones I love.

Chapter Twenty

Ryker

To say I was shocked that Demi actually agreed to come to the clubhouse with me would be an understatement.

The fact she didn't run gives me hope that she is starting to trust me and yet the entire ride there I have to remind myself to manage my expectations. It will take time for her to trust in me enough to give me her truth.

From the tone of that phone call earlier, I'm afraid it's time we don't have.

The thought of invading her privacy, letting Byte loose to delve into her past, leaves a bad taste in my mouth. But really what choice do I have? I'm at a loss of how to move forward if she keeps denying me.

I can physically feel the anxiety rolling off her in waves. It's like a tsunami gaining speed, waves of tension hitting me harder the closer we get to our destination.

Reaching across the console, I lace my fingers with hers, settling our joined hands on my thigh, rubbing circles over her knuckles to soothe her. To bring her anxiety down a level or two.

"It's gonna be okay, Demi." I know she doesn't believe me but she will.

This is my chance to prove to her I am the man she needs. The man that will walk beside her in the light, not leave her standing in my shadow.

Silence engulfs us throughout the rest of the drive. I continue the back and forth movement of my thumb, hoping beyond hope to calm her down by the time we get there.

A few minutes later, I pull up in front of the clubhouse, putting the gear in park, I leave the SUV running for the moment. "Look at me, Firecracker."

Patience will be my friend if I want to win this woman over. Because make no mistake, in this battle of wills we've been engaged in, I won't be satisfied until I have all of her. This is no game to me. I am all in with this woman.

Unfortunately, she's not ready to hear that just yet. I have to play this smart if I want to keep her from running. Carefully execute my battle plan in this war to win her heart.

"I know you're scared. Every instinct in your body telling you to run." I say. "But you gotta trust that I can help you. Every single person, man or woman, in this clubhouse will protect you with their lives."

She huffs out a humorless laugh. "That's what I'm afraid of. I couldn't live with myself if something happens to them." She says but her next words give me hope. Hope that what is happening between us is affecting her as much as me.

"My world would be destroyed if something were to happen to *you*, Ryker." Her voice is so soft, I almost miss the longing in her words.

Bringing our joined hands to my lips, I press a kiss to the back of her fingers. "If that's true, then trust me, Demi. Give me your truth so I'm armed to fight this battle." I press.

Several long seconds pass as I meet her searching gaze unwaveringly, silently conveying the commitment of my promise.

"Okay, Ryker." I didn't realize how tense I was until my muscles go slack at her whisper. Breath expels from my lungs in a relieved sigh so loud they probably hear it in the clubhouse.

"I promise you won't regret this, Firecracker." I tell her between kisses to her knuckles.

"You better be right, Big Guy." The return of her sass releases the last of my tension. Tension I didn't even realize I held onto until my shoulders drop from around my ears.

"Come on. Let's get inside." What I don't tell her is the longer we stay out here in the open, the more I feel like a sitting duck in the idling SUV.

My skin itches at the thought of evil eyes crawling all over us. Dwight would be an idiot to think he can attack us here but my gut screams that the asshole isn't playing with a full deck. Not if he's still hung up on Demi after all this time.

"Wait there." When she looks ready to argue, I again do the one thing I don't do with anyone. "Please, Demi." I am the man that gives orders, used to those orders being followed without question.

Life with Demi is a double-edged sword. The fire I love about her, the fire that makes her my equal, is the one thing I fear will be her downfall in this dangerous game we've unwittingly been pulled into.

But she gives me this. Doing what I ask, her hand drops from the door handle to rest in her lap as I exit the vehicle. Eyes on a swivel, I search our surroundings with deadly intent but the itch is gone. That feeling of being watched missing as I guide Demi through the doors of the clubhouse.

Maybe Dwight is smarter than I gave him credit for.

Chapter Twenty-One

Demi

I second guess my decision to come here even as Ryker hustles me into the clubhouse. Oh, who am I kidding, I've waffled back and forth so many times I feel like a freakin' yo-yo right now.

My biggest fear? Something happening to this man. This wonderfully protective man who would give his life to protect me.

No matter my promise to him, I will do everything in my power to keep that from happening. Up to and including delivering myself right back into Dwight's sadistic hands if it comes down to it because there is nothing worse he could do to me than taking Ryker out of this world. Take him away from me and the people who love him.

In a contest of importance, Ryker has me beat hands down. The people within these walls who rely on him. The people of this town who have grown to trust the MC and the quiet support they provide. They *need* him.

That is the gift of Ryker, the quietly stoic man that expects nothing in return. No recognition. No accolades for what is inherently ingrained in his DNA.

I may be winning hearts with my sweets but in no way does that compare to the integrity of this man. The quiet strength of will he possesses, that he protects his MC family with.

That protective presence surrounds me now as we exit the SUV. The way he walks at my back as we move out in the open, his heat comforting like a baby wrapped in its favorite blanket.

The longing to lean on him, the need to share my burden is overwhelming.

Even now, as he guides me across the main room, heading to the bar to talk to Byte, his hand rests at the small of my back. Every move he makes infuses me with a sense of security. A silent promise that he will do everything in his power to keep me safe.

Glancing over my shoulder, I take a flying leap, trusting Ryker to catch me before I fall flat on my face. "Can we talk in your office?"

His steps falter, freezing smack dab in the middle of the room as he stares down at me. Treats me to that all-knowing intense scrutiny. The hand at my back slips to my hip, a reassuring squeeze delivered discreetly.

"Do you want me to grab Byte first? Or do you want to do this alone?" He asks quietly, proving once again how well he knows me already.

"I think I need to do this in private." I whisper in the nearly empty room.

He changes direction at the seriousness he must see in my expression, leading me down the hallway at a clipped pace.

My nerves riot the closer we get to his office. To the privacy I asked for.

Doubt creeps in with every step we take until it's a bubbling inferno in my belly by the time he closes the door.

God, I don't think I can do this.

There is every possibility that what I'm about to share will change the way Ryker sees me. Where he now looks at me with pride, that can so quickly change to disgust by the end of my tale.

God knows I have enough of that to go around. I've lived with a boatload of self-loathing for so long, it's become downright suffocating.

"Do you want a drink?" Ryker asks from where he leans on his desk.

"No. I'm good." I decline against my better judgement.

Taking a deep breath, I break eye contact, looking away from that too perceptive gaze. There is absolutely no way I'll get my entire embarrassing story out otherwise.

"I was young and dumb." Of course, it sounds like the beginning of any life lesson your parents tell you as a child. A tale of warning. A Lifetime series turned reality.

"I met Dwight when I foolishly decided to take a walk on the wild side. Thought it would be fun to see how the other side lives. Got dressed up and went to the Black Demon's Motorcycle Club." I stop, not sure I can get this all out.

"Shit. I need that drink. I don't know how I thought I could get through this stone cold sober." I laugh bitterly.

Ryker, bless him, doesn't comment but he does move across the room to the bar. He silently pours me a glass of whiskey before returning to my side.

I still can't look at him, my eyes suddenly finding a spot on the wall past his shoulder. I stare at it like it's the most fascinating thing in the room.

He doesn't push me, waiting patiently for me to collect my thoughts. To get my emotions under control.

After a fortifying sip, I continue my sad story. "I thought I hit the jackpot. A hot guy. A biker with a heart of gold? My naïve self thought I found a unicorn.

"In hindsight, I see all the signs. He played the part well, showered me with attention while slowly cutting me off from my friends and family. Controlling the things I did. He decided what I did and didn't wear. Took control of my phone."

The whiskey burns the back of my throat as I stop talking and sling the rest back. My hand trembles as I set the glass down on his desk. It would be so easy to ask for another, a little more liquid courage to finish my sad story.

"The only people in my life that didn't give up on me were my mom and my sister Amy. They pushed me to leave him. To open my eyes to what he was doing but I wouldn't hear a word about it. At least not until it was too late."

I chance a glance up at Ryker and then wished I hadn't. His clenched jaw, the intensity burning in his eyes, he knows precisely how my story will end.

If only I had been as smart.

"He worked fast. We were together less than six months and, in that time, he took almost complete control of my life." I stare out the window, my past playing like scenes from a horror movie in my mind.

"One day I did something to make him mad. Let slip that my mom was trying to talk me into leaving him. So stupid when I look back now. It's not like I was miserable with him, so I thought nothing of mentioning the conversation. Thought he would find the same humor in the idea as me." Boy, how wrong I was.

"That day was the first and last time he hit me. One minute I'm talking about the ridiculousness of leaving and the next I'm on the floor cheek on fire. Thinking how spot on my mom was."

Embarrassment burns my cheeks as I reveal my stupidity to this strong man. A man of integrity who would never even consider doing something so vile. The inherent goodness in Ryker, the strength of character he shows me in our every interaction, I'm an idiot for refusing him. For running scared these last six months, afraid to jump in feet first with him. To give him everything he wanted.

Girl, you haven't learned a damn thing in the past year.

And isn't that a depressing thought?

Chapter Twenty-Two

Ryker

I am going to kill that motherfucker.

My rational mind doesn't give a shit that Demi wasn't mine at the time. Hell, we didn't even know each other then.

Try telling that to my rage, because right now it does not give a shit about any sort of logic.

This woman is *mine*. And the fact some piece of shit thought it was acceptable to place his hands on her? Tried to break the strength of her spirit? That is a mistake that will deliver him to his grave.

The tears streaming down Demi's cheeks break my heart. If that piece of shit wasn't already a dead man walking for laying hands on her, the emotional upheaval he continues to cause would seal his fate.

My rage soars to new levels but I do my best to rein it in. This moment is about her. Lifting the weight of the fear, the embarrassment, the disappointment in herself, from her shoulders. Because right now that shit is stifling her spirit.

If there is one thing I know for sure, Demi is in no way responsible for what happened and I have a feeling this is just the beginning of her story.

Fighting every instinct screaming inside me to pull her close, I restrain myself. She needs to purge the rest of her story if we have any hope of moving forward together.

"What happened next?" The question grinds out, my voice a deep growl thanks to the monster raging inside.

The question breaks her concentration from the window of my office, pulls her from the memories eating her up inside.

"I told him we were done. Left that same day. Moved in with my mom for a few weeks until I got my own place again. I really thought he was done with me. Out of sight, out of mind, you know?" She says sardonically. "But then weird things started happening. At first, I chalked them up to coincidence, wrong numbers when there was only silence on the other end of a call."

She turns back to the window once again. Almost as if she's ashamed of herself for not realizing what was happening.

"Hey, Firecracker." Unable to stomach the distance between us, I step to her, moving right into her personal space. Pulling her close to block her line of sight to the window so she has no choice but to look at me. "Hindsight is always twenty, twenty. Most people wouldn't make the connection until it was too late. You are strong. You left."

Cupping her cheek, I wait for her eyes to meet mine before continuing. "You have *nothing* to be ashamed of. That asshole is the shameful one. Real men don't treat women that way. Only a piece of shit lays hands on his woman."

Her head drops forward until her face is buried in my chest, silent sobs racking her body as her tears soak the fabric of my T-shirt. Helplessness is not a feeling I know well, but in this moment, it is all I've got as I wrap my arms around her, pulling her close to give her the comfort she so desperately needs.

"What did he do to send you running?" I do my best to keep my rage in check, knowing whatever it was had to be bad.

"He broke into my home. Violated my safe space and then thought it would be a riot to call me at the exact moment I saw the destruction. Not only did he break in and destroy my home, but the fact he knew when I would walk in to see it? There was no way he was going to let me get away from him.

"So, I packed what I could fit in my car and fled that night. Left my family to keep them safe. I drove with no destination, just wandered on backroads and no name highways for days. I had no idea what I was going to do." She says.

"But then I got to Tennessee and figured not even Dwight would think to look for me here. So, I started paying attention to my surroundings until I found Frostown. The space for rent on Main Street sold me on it. This was my chance to prove myself. Prove I could make better choices and stand on my own."

God, the strength of character in this woman. Striking out on her own. Even without a psycho ex on her tail? Not many people, man or woman, would be able to succeed like she has in such a short amount of time.

Demi is the kind of person to stand and fight, so he had to have scared the shit out of her to force her into hiding.

Her strength of character, her willingness to sacrifice herself for the ones she loves. It leaves me in awe of her.

"But I wasn't careful enough. He must have been watching my family or he had someone watching them. That's more his speed, letting others do the work for him."

"Joker said something about a family emergency. Did he do something to one of them? Is that why you had to go back?" I ask her.

"No, nothing like that. My mom had a heart attack. She's recovering at home now. Amy said she doesn't want to slow down so my other sister Bianca is staying with her. Making sure she takes it easy." More sobs break free.

I'm gutted as even more tears streak down her face. She's obviously close to her family. Keeping her distance this last year had to have been hard for her.

"She'll be okay, baby. If she's anything like you, she's a fighter." I have nothing to go by but Demi had to have gotten her spirit from somewhere and if what I suspect is true – how desperately she misses her family – then I'm sure I have her mother to thank for the phenomenal woman standing in my arms.

Her arms tighten around my waist, a sense of calm settling over her that has been missing since we met. Even the night she fell asleep on my deck, there was an underlying anxiety simmering just under the surface.

"I need to talk to Byte. *We* need to talk to him. Give him all the intel you have on Dwight so he can start digging into him." I hate to make her relive it again, but I need Byte armed with as much intel as possible.

My gut says the asshole will go underground now that he's made contact. We'll need the advantage if we're gonna win this battle. I have no doubt by the time Byte is done we'll know him better than he knows himself.

Yet my worry is for nothing as the amazing woman in my arms steels her spine and steps away with a nod.

How ironic that if it wasn't for that asshole, I never would have met her. I would still be missing the other half of my soul without even knowing she was out there.

"Okay. Go get him. I'll give him everything I know about Dwight." Her voice is strong this time.

Gone is the embarrassment and shame. At least for now. I'm under no delusion that this one conversation wiped it all away.

It'll take time for her to see what we all see in her. The strength of character, the fiercest of the fierce who will protect those she loves until her dying breath.

Now more than ever, she is exactly the woman I want at my side.

Chapter Twenty-Three

Ryker

"Yep, that about sums it up." From her perch on my lap, Demi finishes a condensed version of her story, giving Byte all the intel she has on her ex.

Through her entire retelling, I've kept my hand on her back. Offering silent support as I trace the tips of my fingers gently up and down her spine. An effort to soothe her, to help her keep a rein on her emotions.

My girl is strong. She wouldn't want to show weakness to anyone else.

The fact she did with me is a sure sign that the trust I have worked so hard to build between us is paying off.

"You need anything else, brother?" I ask Byte who is already vibrating with the need to get his hands on his laptop. To do what he does best, turning his sights on this bastard and digging up every skeleton in his closet. As quickly as possible.

After what went down with Mac's woman, Byte feels responsible for the culprits continued evasion. He's been working nonstop to get a bead on Sarah's ex and he won't stop until he gets his hands on him but I have no doubt he can handle this situation too.

"Naw, man. This should be plenty to get me started." He stands from the chair across from my desk. "Oh, I forgot. The window for the bakery came in. Danger and Mac went to meet the guys to install it. Should be good to go by tomorrow morning."

Demi perks up on my lap. "Great. I am so ready to get back to it."

"Babe, we need to figure this out before you reopen the bakery." I know before I even finish, my words are gonna fall on deaf ears.

My girl is nothing if not independent and to say she's been going stir crazy the past week is an understatement. Even with all the experimentation she's doing with her cakes, her nervous energy grows stronger every day that she's not working in her bakery. The woman has no clue how to stop and take a breather.

"I won't stop living my life, Big Guy. We don't know how long this is going to take and I can't afford to stay closed indefinitely." She argues.

"Besides, you can't keep me a kept woman forever." She huffs while moving to stand.

I stop her with a hand on her thigh.

"Don't. I like you just where you are, Firecracker. And maybe I do like the idea of you waiting for me at home every day." I say just to get a rise out of her.

Before the retort I can see in her eyes falls from her lips, Byte makes a break for the door. "I'm out. Don't need to witness the verbal foreplay about to play out."

"Jerk!" Demi calls out but he just laughs as he disappears through the doorway.

"Baby." I start but she cuts me off with her usual sarcasm.

"Don't even try it, Big Guy." She says. "You are not gonna talk me out of this. I'm going back to work. You can have someone watch out for me. Hell, you can set up shop there yourself if you feel the need but you will not stop me from reopening."

She cups my cheek to soften her words and I can't help tilting my head to lean further into her palm. Reveling in the fact Demi is the one initiating the intimate caress for the first time.

Sex is different. The intimacy of her touch now worth so much more.

"Okay, Firecracker. Give me one more day, at least? I want to talk to the brothers so we're prepared." I say. "I need to make sure you're protected."

Her eyes go soft as she strokes her fingers over my cheek before leaning in to press a soft kiss to my lips.

"Okay. I'll wait one more day but we need to do something. I'm gonna go crazy if I have to sit in that quiet house alone one more night!"

Well shit. She sure does know how to lay on the guilt trip. I know damn well, it's my fault she's been sitting home alone. I've been a coward the last seven days, hiding out at the clubhouse until she goes to bed before sneaking into my own damn house. Shameful for sure.

In my defense, it was the only way to stick to my plan to gain her trust before adding sex to the mix. I can fully admit I probably should have gone about it a little differently.

"You have two choices. We can stay here and catch up with everyone, or we can go home, cook dinner and spend some time together. What do you say?" I ask her.

"Hmm, not sure if dinner together is enough to make up for you avoiding me all week." The lines around her eyes crinkle with her sass, a breathtaking smile gracing her face.

Getting her secrets out lifted a huge weight off her shoulders. Finally, the burden isn't only her own and the relief is evident in her entire demeanor. The loosening of her shoulders. The smiles come easier, what once seemed forced, now lights her up from the inside out.

Burying my face in her neck, I inhale a huge breath of the unique scent that is all Demi. Sugar and spice, just like her personality.

She may have a hard exterior, keeping people at arm's length with her sarcasm, but on the inside she's as soft as a marshmallow.

So irresistible, I don't even try to stop myself from trailing kisses down the side of her neck, rewarded by the shivers racking her body. She's not as unaffected as she's trying to let me think.

"How about I give you an hour to socialize to your heart's content? Then you're all mine for the rest of the night." Sexual promise laces my words, leaving no doubt of my intentions once I get her all to myself.

"Okay, Big Guy. You have yourself a deal." She says but makes no move to stand as I continue exploring.

"And Demi?" Wrapping my hand around her neck, I bury my fingers in the hair at the back of her head, tightening just enough to grab her attention.

From the dilating of her pupils and the squirming of her ass on my lap, she loves it.

I wait until her eyes focus back on me before I speak again. "I'll be counting down the minutes until you're all mine."

Chapter Twenty-Four

Demi

I feel lighter, freer. My laugh comes easier. More carefree as I chat with the men and women of the club.

Sarah and I catch up. She's dying of curiosity, wanting to know everything about my family. I don't censor my words, answering her questions about my past.

The only topic I steer clear of is Dwight. That's a story for a different day but I do tell her about my mom and my sisters. I didn't realize just how much I ached to share them with others. People that don't know them but truly seem to want to learn more about me.

I'm still sarcastic, because hello that's just who I am, but the jokes lack their usual snark. I sneak one or two self-deprecating remarks in without the underlying self-loathing.

If there was a lingering sense of worry that people would look at me differently, it was for nothing as every single person here has treated me the same as they always have.

Maybe even better since Ryker stays glued to my side through it all. It's a nice change from his usual post across the room, glare firmly in place, daring any man to step up to me and tempt his wrath.

And the entire time, his touch lingers. A hand on my back, brushing a loose curl behind my ear, leaning down to rain soft kisses over my shoulder. Everywhere I am, he is too. His scent surrounds me. Potently sexual. Downright irresistible.

The man has kept my arousal on simmer all night. Every time he guided me to the dance floor. Pulled me into his arms, his body moving in an erotic imitation of the naked dance I fully expect tonight. He knows what he's doing and is glorying in my body's response.

I stick to one drink over the hour Ryker promised me. I want to be stone cold sober for the naughty times he has in store for us when I finally get him all to myself.

We dance. We laugh. We catch up with good friends. The family Ryker has made here exactly what my heart was searching for and I didn't even know it. Every person present obvious in their respect and love for him even when he cuts our time short. When he decides he's ready for our time alone, he about drags me off the dance floor and away from the bar before I can get caught up in another conversation with the girls.

"Demi!" My bestie calls as she walks through the doors with her man Mac. She tears her hand from his, rushing across the room to wrap me in a hug. *God, I've missed her.*

"Girl aren't you a sight for sore eyes. I've missed you!" I have no problem telling her. Kate broke through my walls the day I met her and I'm super lucky to have her in my life.

"I missed you too. Don't ever leave like that again without telling me." She pulls away to throw her version of a stern look my way.

I burst out laughing at the adorability of it. My girl is definitely a gentle soul. Ryker gets pulled away by Mac, some excuse about checking out his bike. I smell a setup here and if the deviousness on my bestie's face is anything to go by, I'm about to get the interrogation of my life.

"So, you and Ryker huh?" She asks with a cat that ate the canary smile. "Did you finally wear him down or did you admit there is more between you two than sexual tension?"

Her eyebrows wiggle across her forehead like a break dancer performing a poorly executed worm. I can't help but laugh at her antics.

"Girl, please don't ever do that again!" My laughter bursts out with a serenity I haven't experienced in well over a year.

"What?" She asks with a frown. "I've been practicing that and everything. Mac says I've got it down."

"Yeah, I don't think so, friend. He was probably just trying to get in your pants." I burst her bubble.

She turns accusing eyes to where her man walks back through the doors with heat tingeing her cheeks. "Darn it. I should have known he had an ulterior motive."

Even through my humor, my eyes are all for the man at his side as they cross the room to us. Kate's question completely forgotten until she pulls my attention back to her.

"Demi, you're not getting out of this. I will make you talk to me with him standing right next to you if I have to." She warns me.

"I don't know, Kate." I give her honesty. "I don't want anything to happen to him. If I let him get too close, there's a good chance of that happening."

"This have something to do with your past?" My friend is too perceptive for my own good.

Reluctantly, I answer her before the men reach us. "Yeah, it does and I'm not ready to talk about it just yet."

"Well, that's not good enough." She says. "I'll give you a couple days, but then I'll be at our regular table at the bakery at closing time. Then all bets are off. You're my best friend and I will be there for you whether you're ready or not."

Emotion clogs my throat. Instead of trying to force any words out, I reach over and wrap her in a bear hug. It takes a minute but I get myself under control enough to speak.

"Okay, bestie. It's a date." I whisper before pulling away just in time for the men to join us.

Ryker gives me a curious look but thankfully doesn't comment.

"You ready, Firecracker? I think it's about time to hold up your end of our bargain." He wraps his arm around my waist, hand settling possessively on my lower back.

That move alone? My arousal bursts right back to the surface, shivers radiating out from the heat of his palm.

A nod is the only action I am capable of and even that takes a herculean effort.

Spoken words? Yeah, right. There is no way my brain can form coherent thoughts and he isn't even touching bare skin yet.

Oh boy, I think my world is about to be rocked and I am all for it.

Hand still at my back, Ryker guides me across the room with intention.

Joker steps in our path before we reach the door with a seriousness he's usually lacking. "Prez, we need to talk."

"Not now, Joker. I know what you want to talk about and I'm not gettin' into it with you tonight. I'll be back in the morning. You can bitch me out then."

Ryker makes a move to go around him but Joker sidesteps to keep pace with him.

"I mean no disrespect, Prez but this can't wait." Joker argues.

"Yes, it can." Ryker has the patience of a saint.

I totally would have kneed him in the balls to get him out of the way by now. But that might have something to do with the anticipation sizzling through my veins. Ryker has kept me on edge all night and I am so ready to collect on his promise.

"You got a problem with Sarah returning to the bakery, you take it up with her, Joker." Ryker bites out, the first indication he may not be as patient as I thought.

Seems he's as impatient to get to the sexy times as me but his words make me pause.

Moving between the two men, I set my hand on Joker's chest to break the stare down between them. "Joker, you know I wouldn't do anything to put Sarah at risk. I care about her too and I would fire her in a heartbeat if that's what it takes to keep her safe. Ryker will have protection on the bakery before we even reopen. You don't have worry about something happening."

I pat his chest at the minute softening of his expression then step back to Ryker's side. I lean into his warmth when he wraps his arm around my waist, pulling me around until my back rests against his chest.

"Like I said, we'll talk tomorrow, Joker." Ryker says. "You have my word, we'll have a plan to protect them before they even step foot back in the bakery."

The slight tilting of Joker's head is about all the agreement he's going to give at this point. This time when Ryker goes to step around him, he allows him to pass and guide me out into the dark night.

Chapter Twenty-Five

Demi

Ryker must have had one of the brothers bring his motorcycle over from the house because it now sits in his usual spot in front of the clubhouse.

Nerves shoot through my belly. It's not like I haven't been on the back of his bike before, but this time is different. Going into this thing with eyes wide open is scary, allowing myself to be vulnerable with a man again? Scary AF.

As we approach his bike, I take a deep breath, capturing the air in my lungs to calm my rioting nerves.

Girl, this is Ryker. He isn't going to do anything to bring you harm. Physically or emotionally.

I watch as he mounts the black beast, mouth turning to dust at the raw masculinity of his movements. He takes his seat as confidently as he runs his club, exuding that aura of control that makes my lady parts stand up and pay attention.

Shaking those wanton thoughts out of my head, I step up to the bike, setting my hand on his shoulder before swinging my short leg over the seat.

His big body doesn't leave much room so I scoot as close as I can, wrapping my arms around his solid waist. I settle my hands on the hard planes of his abs, abs I know are perfectly defined. A girl's wet dream if I'm being completely honest.

The engine purrs beneath us as Ryker takes the winding roads home. It's been a while since I've been on the back of a motorcycle and immediately, I get lost in the euphoria, the trust I've placed in this steady man.

Even in the dark, the beauty of our surroundings relaxes me. Maybe even more so than in the light of day. There's a mystery to what hides in the dark just beyond the light of the motorcycle

All too soon, Ryker rolls into his garage. Shutting off the engine, we sit for a moment. Ever since he brought me here, I've come to realize that I enjoy the comforting silence when I share it with this man. My normally on the move mentality quiet when I'm with him.

"You gonna get off, Firecracker?" There's a note of humor in his voice. I don't need to see his face to recognize the smile gracing those beautiful lips.

"Hmm. I hope so, Big Guy." The words shoot out without thought. I just can't help myself. I do love to rile him up.

And, yep from the smoldering look he shoots over his shoulder, I've accomplished my goal.

"Baby, you'll be gettin' off until you can't take any more if you can unglue your ass from this seat and get inside the house."

Oh my, I think my panties just burst into flames.

I give a gentle squeeze to his stomach before raising my hands to his shoulders, using the strength of his muscles to lift myself up to dismount the bike.

Entering the house, Ryker backs me right up to the closed door. Forearms braced against the hard wood, he cages me in much like I longed for all those months ago. Muscles rippling, his big body overwhelms all my senses.

"This isn't just sex, Demi. We do this and you're mine. You ready for that?"

The seriousness of his words, the intensity in his gaze, he's a hundred percent serious. Ready to commit even after learning about my past. About all my bad decisions.

The walls around my heart crack. Absolutely shatter as I study his beautiful face. For whatever reason this amazing man still wants me. Still sees a future with me. Does the thought scare me? Abso-freakin-lutely.

But still, I'm ready to take the chance. Take a chance to trust my judgement even after all the mistakes of my past. Maybe even because of them.

I'd like to think I'm smarter this time around and if there's one thing I've learned from this man, it's that we all make mistakes. What matters is the way in which we rally, the way we draw on those experiences for self-growth. To continually build strength of character. That is what truly defines us.

So, I'm ready to take a chance to trust Ryker. Believe in the man he's shown me since the night we met at Dean's Bar. The loyalty, patience and understanding.

I desperately want to believe I found my unicorn when I wasn't even looking. Wrapping my arms around his neck, I lean up on the tips of my toes to meet his gaze head on. Well as head on as I can with our height difference.

"Don't make me regret this, Big Guy." I warn him before nipping his bottom lip. With eyes wide open, I tease him. Lick across the spot to soothe the ache from my sharp teeth.

And then Ryker takes the control completely out of my hands, arms around my waist, he pulls me close. So close, we're pressed together from chest to knees.

My breasts crushed to the hard planes of his pecs, the movement rubs my nipples erotically behind the lace of my bra and the sensual abrasion feels oh so good.

An embarrassing squeak of surprise bursts out when he catches my ass in his hands, lifting until I have no choice but to wrap my legs around his waist.

Locking my ankles at his back, I hold on for the ride as he carries me up the staircase. His steps solid even as he continues to explore. Torturous nips of his teeth followed by long licks to the sensitive column of my neck. I feel his touch in every nerve ending in my body.

That's gonna leave a mark.

His footsteps echo as he enters his bedroom, soft light from the window casts dancing shadows over the bed as he closes the distance.

With a tenderness I don't expect from this gruff man, he places me in the middle of the mattress, following me down until he hovers over me. All that leashed power surrounding me.

And there he stays. For a full minute, he stares, studying me. He must see what he's looking for because he leans down, taking my mouth in a scorching kiss.

My God, this man's mouth. The things he can do with it. My pussy spasms at the thought of all that potent intensity focused on my aching core. I'm afraid I may not survive the experience.

A sharp bite to my bottom lip snaps me back to the moment. "What are you thinking about so hard, Firecracker?"

My cheeks heat as I consider how much to share.

Go for it, girl. You know this man will rock your world. All you have to do is ask.

"I was thinking how good you are with your mouth." Is the heater on? It sure feels like the house is heating up. My cheeks are downright blazing.

A knowing smirk tilts one side of his mouth. "Oh yeah? Wondering how good it'll feel in other places? Here maybe?" The heat of his palm burns right through my clothes as he cups my pussy, a teasing pressure meant to drive me crazy.

"You all talk, Big Guy? Or you actually gonna show me?" Raising my head, I sink my teeth into his full lower lip, keeping my eyes glued to his as I suck the flesh into my mouth.

Eyes flaring, he pulls back until I'm forced to release his lip with a loud pop. And then he swoops in, mouth taking mine in an erotic caress. Our tongues duel, a silent battle of wills. A challenge for dominance I have no problem losing. Am eagerly anticipating the reward of my surrender.

My head drops back to the pillow, neck no longer able to hold me up as he chases, devouring my mouth. He dominates me, tongue thrusting in an imitation of the erotic act we're inevitably heading to.

Whimpers fall from my lips, silently begging for more. Hands lifting, I tunnel my fingers into the hair at the back of his head, holding him to me.

In no time at all, my clothes disappear, the man a magician as he strips me without breaking the connection of our mouths except to lift my shirt over my head.

I don't even realize I'm completely naked until he leans back on his heels to admire his handy work. His hands cup my breasts, fingers torturing my nipples, those all-seeing eyes catching my body's every reaction.

And when he leans down to suck one of my nipples into his mouth, my back shoots off the bed, forcing my sensitive flesh even further into his mouth.

His busy hands trace over my curves. Exploring down my ribcage, mapping the roundness of my hips. His journey ends at the juncture of my thighs.

My already spread legs gives him the perfect opportunity to tease my pussy as cream flows freely, soaking his fingers where he plays with my clit. It would be downright embarrassing if I wasn't so caught up in the sensations he evokes. Coherent thought an impossibility.

His big body moves down, lips gliding over the ticklish skin of my belly. He leaves me squirming as his tongue traces from one hipbone to the other.

Hips lifting, I chase that devilish mouth, urging him to move faster. To soothe the fire he's stoked in my pussy. But he refuses to be rushed, stubbornly maintaining that slow agonizing pace as he savors me.

"Patience, baby. Good things come to those who wait." How can he taunt me at a time like this? Does he have any idea what he's doing to me?

"Screw patience, Ryker. I think you've made me wait long enough. I want you to fuck me." Frustration coats my words. I am so far beyond taking it slow it's laughable.

And the bastard knows it. Has the audacity to laugh in the face of my demand.

"It's cute you think you have the control here, baby." His words whisper over my core, mouth so close to where I need him.

"I'm hungry and since you failed to feed me, I'm gonna gorge myself on this pretty little pussy."

Oh God.

Then his mouth is on me. Wet slurping sounds fill the room, so much so I might have been self-conscious if I could think beyond chasing the building pleasure.

Ryker *devours* my pussy like an all you can eat buffet. Fingers, teeth, tongue. He uses them all to drive me wild, pressing my thighs wide, holding me immobile to his erotic torment until he pushes me right over the edge.

His name screams past my lips as my orgasm hits. Lights explode, the world tilts and I can do nothing but take it. The sweetest kind of torture as I take everything he has to give.

Breath pants past my lips as the pressure of his mouth softens to slow licks circling my clit. Keeping my desire alive as I recover.

His hands retreat, the sound of his belt releasing, the zipper of his jeans loud in the room as he releases his cock while sliding up my body. Face to face, he stares me down, lips glistening with the proof of my arousal.

"Delicious." He growls as he lines himself up with my opening.

The image we must make. This dominant man fully clothed, playing my body like a finely tuned instrument. He knows all the tricks to make my body sing. Who would have thought *this* was my fantasy? The dominant hand, his controlling ways. It all serves to bring me right back to the edge when his cock breaches the lips of my pussy.

The burning stretch of his entry. The fullness to almost overflowing. It hurts in the best possible way.

"God, Demi. So wet, baby." He grinds out. "You take me so good. You feel how good we fit together? Your pussy is strangling my cock."

Tightening my legs around his waist, I pull myself up, chasing his mouth. He meets me head on to fight for control.

"Harder. I need more, Ryker." I'm not above begging. Happily relinquishing the power, the control, into his capable hands.

And what glorious hands they are, squeezing my ass, lifting my hips to a new angle. Rewarding my surrender, the head of his cock hits the exact place I need to see stars.

"Right there. Don't stop. Please don't stop." I plead.

And boy does he give me just what I need. Hips pistoning, he *takes* me. Right to the edge of euphoria, and the best part, he flies right into the stratosphere with me.

My name a growl rumbling through his chest, his thrusts turn frantic until he freezes deep inside me. My pussy weeps at the perfect fullness, muscles contracting through my orgasm.

My legs fall to the sides, arms flop to the bed. I'm a boneless heap of sparking nerve endings as he collapses on top of me. Our bodies slip and slide, sticky with sweat.

He lifts his head, presses a soft kiss to my lips. "I knew it would be explosive." Laughter bursts out, washing over us as our bodies cool. Heartbeats return to normal. And the unmistakable masculine pride in his words is adorable.

"Alright, Big Guy. Don't let it go to your head. It was okay." Sassing him is second nature.

His hands attack, fingers digging into my sides as giggles escape me. "Ryker, stop!" I force out between gasping breaths.

"Seriously, baby? You really think you can say that shit and get away with it? Just okay my ass." He playfully snarls down at me.

Fingers on the move, he slips a hand between our bodies. The agonizing squeeze of my clit between two fingers brings an immediate end to my humor as moans replace my giggles.

"Ryker. No, I can't take anymore." But my body betrays my words as my hips lift, muscles contracting around his hardening cock still buried deep inside me.

"I don't think so, baby. You wanna play? I can play all night." He whispers against my lips.

Then he proceeds to show me just how *good* he can play until I pass out from exhaustion as the sun begins to rise.

Chapter Twenty-Six

Ryker

After giving an abbreviated version of Demi's story, my gaze circles the table, carefully studying the reaction of every single member in the room.

When my eyes land on Joker, I linger a little longer, watching as the fury within bubbles to the surface. If the brother clenches his jaw any tighter, he's gonna need a crowbar to pry it loose.

His fury is twofold. He has his own demons when it comes to domestic violence stemming from his childhood. Add in the fact that the situation puts Sarah in harm's way, it's easy to see the brother is ready to blow and not in a good way.

"Relax, Joker. We got a plan. Two of us, minimum, will be on the bakery at all times. We won't let anything happen to Sarah or Demi. We've got them covered." I reassure him, unfazed by the fury rolling off him in waves.

"Brother, don't go doin' nothing stupid." Mac warns him. "I can see it brewing in your eyes. You try to lock Sarah down? She's never gonna forgive your sorry ass."

"Fuck off, Mac. It ain't your woman in danger here." Joker spits the biting words at him.

"She isn't your woman, jackass. Or did I miss you growing some balls and claiming her?" Mac taunts him.

Joker launches himself out of his chair, lunging at Mac before any of us can stop him. Not that we try. No, we all sit back and enjoy the show, knowing damn good and well the brother needs to blow off some steam.

It's been a long time coming with all that bottled up frustration. Sarah has had him on the hook since day one and the patience needed to take things slow with the wounded woman is taking its toll.

Bomber finally steps in when the two roll under the table, knocking into chairs between grunts and flying fists.

"That's all you got, asshole?" Mac yells while struggling to break free of Bomber's hold as he drags him off Joker. Both of them got some good shots in. They'll definitely be getting some loving care from their women tonight.

"That's enough!" The pound of my fist echoes off the table and around the room.

"You all know what to do." I make eye contact with each and every brother before settling back on Joker. "Joker, it'll be you and me tomorrow morning. There's safety in numbers so we ride in together."

This way I can keep an eye on him. Make sure he doesn't lose his shit and do something stupid.

"Byte is still looking for the asshole. Until we get new intel, I want every single one of you on high alert. I don't trust this piece of shit not to go after someone close to Demi if he can't get his hands on her." I warn them.

Ready to call an end to this meeting, I'm anxious to return to the sleeping beauty in my bed. She was knocked out hard when I woke up this morning, adorable little snores falling from her lips. I couldn't stomach the thought of waking her up and now I hope like hell she's right where I left her.

I did leave a note in case she woke up while I was gone, but really hoping she hasn't stirred from her peaceful slumber. The though of sliding in bed, and right back into her warm pussy is all the motivation I need to finish this meeting ASAP.

A commotion from the main room sounds before I can dismiss everyone. A fist bangs on the door like the cops have come calling.

"Dammit, Ryker! I know you're in there." Demi's furious voice reverberates through the rafters. Well damn, my plan to pick up where we left off goes right up in smoke.

Every head at the table swivels simultaneously as all the brothers turn to me with wide-eyed looks.

"Ruh oh. I think someone's in trouble." Joker's good mood returns at the worst possible moment.

I'm up and out the door in a split second, a million worst case scenarios running through my head, no clue what could be wrong.

I stop short in the doorway when I catch sight of a fuming Demi. Arms crossed, propping those gorgeous breasts up like an offering, her foot taps away on the wood floor.

My T-shirt swallows her whole. If she's wearing shorts, I can't tell. All I can say is she damn well better not be walking around without them in front of my brothers.

They may not care about putting on a show to get off but that just isn't me. Never has been and *never* will be with Demi.

'What's wrong, Demi?" I run my hands up and down her arms, around her body, searching for any sign of injury. "Did something happen? How did you get here?"

The questions spit out rapid fire, my heart rate spiking. I never should have left her alone in the house. The fact there were men watching her doesn't mean a damn thing right now.

"What's wrong?" She screeches, sweeping all that beautiful hair over one shoulder, exposing the love bite I left on the beautiful column of her neck.

"Do you see this? I can't work with this, Ryker! I work with the public. In a *small town*. Everyone is gonna be talking about this." Chest heaving, she's standing toe to toe with me by the end of her rant.

To be honest, I can't think of a damn thing beyond how beautiful she is in her rage. Despite the fact it's aimed my way. Hell, maybe even because of that. I'm a sick bastard, I know.

"Um, Demi. You'd have to be blind not to see that big ass hickey. They can probably see Prez's mark from the space station." Joker chimes in unhelpfully, coming to stand by me side.

"Nice work, man." He raises his hand for a fist bump.

All it takes is the smack of my hand to the back of his head to shut the dumbass up. One I happily deliver sightlessly, not once taking my eyes off the furious temptress fuming in front of me.

This is what I wanted. The woman willing to stand up to me. No matter what. Insignificant or not, Demi is a firecracker and will call me on my shit.

Although, I can't really say I'm sorry for marking my territory. Masculine pride sparks to life and she must see it on my face. Her eyes fire blue flames my way, narrowed in on the smirk I feel lifting my lips.

Stifled laughter comes from behind us before Mac cautions me. "Bro, you may want to tone that shit down a little. She's about to blow and she's standing a little too close to your junk for any of our comfort."

I see it, the moment the thought crosses her mind. In a nanosecond, I've got her thrown over my shoulder, hand on her ass to confirm she does indeed have shorts on under my shirt.

Leaving my hand right where it is, I use my hold to keep her from squirming right out of my arms. I want her fired up, not hurt because she lost control.

With a sharp smack to the supple flesh filling my palm, I warn her. "Hold still, Firecracker. You hurt yourself and I'm really gonna have to spank that ass."

Her squirming may stop, but her tiny fists beat on my back the entire way to my office at the back of the clubhouse.

"You bastard! Put me down!" Thankfully her screech is somewhat muffled by the fabric of my T-shirt. Still, doors open up and down the hall at the commotion. People cautiously poke their heads out, mostly the women that couldn't make it to our earlier meeting.

"Demi? Are you okay?" Sarah's hesitant voice freezes Demi mid-attack. Worry for her friend laces her voice. Lily and little Joey do their best to peek around their mom's legs, a captivated audience to Demi's shenanigans.

Demi props herself up as much as she can with her palms on my back. "Oh, hey guys. I'm fine. Just a little disagreement." She reassures her.

"Oh, okay. If you're sure." Sarah isn't quite ready to let it go.

"Yep, we're good. I'll see you at the bakery bright and early tomorrow." I don't even try to hide my snort. The woman could sweeten an entire batch of pastries with the sugar dripping from her voice.

I continue my trek down the hall when Joker rounds the corner, no doubt on his way to soothe Sarah's nerves.

The slam of the door echoes through my office as Demi's renews her efforts to maim me once the barrier is in place.

"Stop it, Firecracker." The smack of my hand to her ass is satisfying in the quiet room. "I'm gonna let you go but you gotta calm down."

"Fine." A puff of hot air bathes my back from the force of her huff where she hangs over my shoulder.

Setting her feet on the floor, my hands massage the globes of her ass where I'm sure I left my mark.

Not gonna lie, the thought of that is just about as satisfying as seeing my mark on her neck for all the world to see.

This woman is *mine* and I want everyone to know it.

Was it a conscious decision to do it? Not really, but that doesn't stop the masculine pride from surging once again when I catch sight of my handiwork.

"Just stop, Big Guy." She warns. "This is so not something to be proud of. Everyone is gonna be talking about me. Wondering who I let defile me."

A burst of laughter escapes at her words. "Defiled you? Baby, this is the twenty-first century. Nobody thinks that way anymore."

"This is a small town, Ryker. They're still stuck in their ways. Thinking women shouldn't be deflowered until marriage. The things I hear in the bakery? Believe me, they'll be talking."

Her arms cross mutinously, once again propping those firm breasts up like an offering.

It takes a whole lot of effort to drag my eyes back up to her face, seeing how serious this is for her.

Crowding her back against the door, I slide the tip of my finger gently over the offending spot. "I'm sorry, baby. It wasn't a conscious decision to mark you. I lose my head when I'm with you."

She uncrosses her arms to wrap them around my waist, resting her chin on my chest to stare up at me. "What am I supposed to do? I can't hold off opening the bakery until this thing fades."

"Go see Jade. She has some shit she uses to hide her tattoos when she needs to. Covers them right up. You wouldn't even know she has them if you didn't know her." Pressing a kiss to her forehead, I step back and gently pull her away from the door.

"You good now?" I ask her.

One side of her mouth tilts up in a smirk. "Not sure. I guess we'll see after I go see Jade." And then the sassy woman throws me a wink over her shoulder as she saunters out of my office.

Something tells me I just got played. Big time.

And I am not mad about it. Not one bit.

Chapter Twenty-Seven

Demi

I knew the vultures would descend the minute I reopened my doors. There was a line at the door a half hour before we opened and the crowd has shown no sign of slowing.

Sarah, bless her, has been running all day but my girl is calm under the pressure. Serving customers quickly and efficiently as I hustle back and forth between the kitchen and the counter, an unending struggle to keep the pastry case full.

We were sold out by noon and had to turn people away until Sarah made the executive decision to lock the doors. Despite the fact our customers had an ulterior motive, nothing can kill the good vibes I have going on while we wipe down the counter and the pastry case.

Even the surge of nosy townsfolk in and out the doors all day wasn't enough of a distraction from Ryker's commanding presence where he sits at Kate's usual table in the corner.

Not once has the man taken his eyes off me even as his phone rang nonstop. Each and every time I walked through the door from the back that intense gaze was locked on me. Tracking my every move. Arousal has been on a slow simmer in my belly all freakin' day.

His stare so potent, I almost ran smack dab into the doorframe the first time I caught him watching me. And wouldn't that have been embarrassing as hell. I might as well have posted a sign on the front door. 'Ryker defiled Demi.'

That sure would have given the busy bodies fodder for their next gossip sesh at the diner.

Although with the way his eyes tracked me all day, it wouldn't take a genius to solve that not-so-secret mystery.

Speaking of the sexy man, I can't help but provoke the bear from the safety of the counter. "You doing okay there, Big Guy? Need anything?"

Leaning my elbows on the counter, I give him a clear shot down the front of my Sweet Treats T-shirt.

"Careful, Firecracker. I have no problem *defiling* you right here for all the world to see." He says behind the lip of his coffee cup. No shame in his game, his eyes are zeroed in on the show I'm giving him.

Jesus, the man is sex on a stick and he damn well knows it. Arousal flushing my cheeks, I glance at Sarah. The poor girl's gaze bounces between us like a fast-paced ping pong match. She makes no effort to hide her fascination with the show playing out.

"You need anything before you go?" It takes a ton of effort to tear my attention away from the irresistible man.

"Um, I think I'm good. Joker is pulling his bike around from the back so I'm going to head out unless you need anything else." She says with heat firing her cheeks.

"Hold on, Sarah. Wait for him to come back in and walk you out." Ryker orders from his seat across the room.

"Okay." She hurries to the back like her ass is on fire, presumably to get her purse. Although it might have something to do with the sexual tension so thick you could cut it with a knife.

As far as I know, my girl hasn't dated since moving in with the MC and something tells me Joker has no problem scaring off any possible suitors. All while biding his time to make a move of his own. Hell, he probably revels in the fear he incites in any idiot dumb enough to shoot his shot with her.

A minute later, the man himself saunters through the door. The intensity of his expression as his eyes eat my friend right up could rival that of Ryker when he's got me in his sights. The potent testosterone in the room is stifling as both men light up the space with their intensity.

"Bye, Demi. I'll see you tomorrow." Bless my friend, she is completely blind to the blazing possessiveness in Joker's eyes.

"See ya tomorrow. Bright and early!" Who am I to burst her bubble? I have a feeling she'd be running scared if she knew even half of what that man feels for her. It's evident in the hand he places at her back, treating her as if she's made of spun gold.

Ryker trails them to the door, turning the lock at their exit.

"That man would wrap her in bubble wrap if he thought he could get away with it." I joke as Ryker turns back to me.

Smoldering intensity burns in his eyes as he stalks me across the room. "I don't want to talk about them right now."

Oh boy. I might be in trouble here.

But I'll be damned if I let it show.

"What do you think you're doing, Big Guy?" I would have gotten away with the blasé question if my skyrocketing pulse, my panted breaths, didn't give me away.

It's stupid really how this man affects me. How he can get me from zero to a hundred in no time flat is ridiculous.

His feet carry him to the counter where he stops directly across from me. His height gives him leverage to lean over and slide his face up the sensitive skin of my neck.

"Hmm, you smell delicious, Firecracker." His voice is gravel, hitting me right in my sweet spot. "So sweet. It's like you bathe in sugar and spice."

"Maybe I do." The comeback is a struggle to push past my lips.

Pulling back, he stares me down. Satisfaction written all over his face at the dumbstruck expression I'm sure is plastered across mine.

"Do you have any frosting in the kitchen, Firecracker?" His mouth drifts back to my neck, those softly whispered words feathering over my ear before he sinks his teeth into the lobe.

Wait, what?

If that isn't a suspicious question from the man that *never* indulges his sweet tooth, I don't know what is.

"Frosting? Why?" My words are cautious.

"Just craving something sweet." He says, pulling back to trace the tips of his fingers over my cheek then dragging his thumb along my bottom lip.

"Oh, yeah. I have some leftover from this morning." I say then give into temptation, sucking the tip of his thumb into my mouth.

Eyes flaring, he slowly draws the digit away then pushes off the counter, standing to his full height. "Lead the way, baby."

In head scratching confusion, I turn to do just that, curious to see what he has up his sleeve. Opening the fridge, I rise to the tips of my toes to reach the top shelf.

Before I can wrap my hand around the airtight container, Ryker is right there, invading my personal space. Front plastered to my back, his hard cock nestles into the seam of my ass as he reaches up to grab the container.

"Pull your hair down and go sit on the counter." He takes a step back while barking the order as he glances around the kitchen. What he's searching for, I have no idea.

Oh God. What is this devious man up to?

I move to the counter and hop on, fighting the urge to question him. So deliciously curious to see what he's up to.

"Take off your shirt but leave the bra." He instructs as he moves around the kitchen, pulling a metal spatula from the drawer next to me.

My eyes flare wide as understanding dawns. By the time I figure out what he's up to, he's back in front of me. Without the safety of the counter to separate us, he steps right up between my spread thighs. The ridge of his hard on a delicious pressure right to my clit. So good I fight back the moan that will expose how much his nearness affects me.

"I'm waiting, baby." My hands snap to motion at the sternness of his words, lifting my shirt over my head and releasing my long hair from the bun at the back of my neck.

And all the while, he watches me. Opening the lid, he dips the spatula into the frosting then brings it to my mouth. "Open."

I do as I'm told. Lips parting, I'm rewarded by the rumble of approval vibrating deep within his chest as he slides the frosting onto my tongue.

He swiftly closes the distance before my mouth closes to savor the chocolate melting on my tongue.

His mouth slams down to mine, velvety tongue thrusting inside to tangle with my own. The heady combination of chocolate and Ryker's unique flavor bursts on my taste buds. And what an enticing combination it is.

Far too soon, he backs off, dropping the spatula in the bowl for the moment. He palms my breasts, massaging and kneading my flesh. Building my desire at lightning speed as his fingers torture my nipples oh so deliciously.

Shockwaves of pleasure burst through my body, radiating all the way down to my toes.

Moans fall from my lips at the look of steady concentration on his face, solely focused on the task at hand. A man on a mission to drive me out of my damn mind.

Once he's satisfied with his handiwork – my nipples hard little points poking through the lace of my bra – his nimble fingers slip inside the lace cups. The drag of the material an erotic friction as he pulls it down until my breasts are plumped up obscenely.

Chancing a look down, the carnal visual is one I will never forget. And when he uses the now cold spatula to spread frosting to the hard tips, a harsh inhale leaves me choking on the saliva pooling in my mouth.

The loud clang of metal is background noise as he drops the spatula to the counter at my hip. Hand pressed to the center of my chest, Ryker forces me back until I'm laid out in front of him.

His tongue darts out. Licking and nibbling one chocolate covered nub until it's glistening before sucking it into his mouth. At the same time, those big hands of his make quick work of the button and zipper of my pants.

And then he's there. Right where I need him most, his fingers swooping in to play my pussy perfectly.

My now clean nipple releases from his mouth with a pop, standing at attention and begging for more. His lips blaze a trail of fire through the valley of my breasts to pay the same dedicated attention to my neglected flesh.

He savors me like a death row inmate devouring his last meal. Groans rumble through his chest. My moans echo through the room as he slides two fingers into my pussy, thumb drifting back and forth over my sensitive clit.

"You taste so good, baby. You gonna come for me?" His hot breath blows over my nipple, turning the tight bud impossibly harder.

"Ryker. Please!" I don't even know what I'm begging for. My brain is completely fried from this salacious game.

Then all thoughts flee as my body soars to the stars. I scream through my orgasm. Incoherent sounds fall from my lips as a tsunami of pleasure blanks my mind.

Long minutes later, I find my voice at last.

"You are definitely a distraction, Big Guy." I tease him as I float down from the high of my orgasm.

His laugh bursts out. The beautiful sound wafting air over my still erect nipples. Turning his head, he rests his chin in the valley between my breasts. Those emerald orbs lock on me, expression full of masculine pride.

"You good? You looked like you needed a little stress relief." He teases right back.

"I don't think I can move my legs. Give me a minute here, buddy. I think you broke me."

I'm rewarded with a full-blown laugh this time. It rumbles from deep in his chest, a delicious friction over my still sensitive breasts. The sight of this strong man dropping the stoic façade, stunning smile spreading his lips.

He is breathtaking in this unguarded moment.

I did that.

Yep, I'm pretty damn proud of myself.

I'd pat myself on the back if I could reach.

Chapter Twenty-Eight

Ryker

My concentration is for shit today. I should have known leaving Demi's protection in another brother's hands would fuck with my head. Not that I don't trust them. Every member of my club would protect Demi with their life if it came down to it.

It's my frustration with the infuriating woman driving me mad. I really thought we had a breakthrough when she opened up to me, but she's been distant the last couple of days. Quiet even and I have no idea what's going through her head.

For every step forward, I feel like we take two giant steps back. It's frustrating as hell and I'm about fed up with it.

"I got nothing on his current location, Prez. This guy is a ghost." Byte admits, pulling my attention back to where he sits on the other side of my desk.

"Any chance of tracing the phone call?" I ask him but he's already shaking his head.

"It was a burner. No way to trace it."

"Shit. Not what I was hoping to hear." I admit with a sigh. "What about his history?"

"Born and raised in northern California. A small town just north of Sacramento. Started getting in trouble early on. In and out of juvie from age thirteen."

He glances at his laptop before continuing. "Did a stint in prison, released at twenty-one. Got hooked up with the Black Demon's while he was inside. For protection, most likely. One of their officers was doing a ten-year bid for dealing drugs but rumor has it they're into a whole lot worse than that."

"What kinds of things?" I ask, really not liking what I'm hearing so far.

"Loan sharking. Running scams out of casinos on the border in Nevada. Prostitution and not always voluntary if you get my meaning."

"How the fuck did Demi get wrapped up with this piece of shit?" It's a rhetorical question. One Byte has the good sense not to answer.

"The assholes started expanding east the last few years. Not quite to Tennessee but they have a chapter in Texas. Been set up there for about two years."

"Anything else I need to know?" I ask, ready to get back to my woman. An urgency to lay eyes on her firing my blood.

"That's the Cliffs Notes version but I'll keep digging. Into both him and the club. We might have more to worry about than a psycho ex. My gut feeling is they're looking for an ideal location for another chapter a little too close for comfort.

"Pattern shows they find a rural area with an established club. Start sending their guys in to stir shit up and force them out of town. If that's the case, Frostown might be on their radar now." He cautions.

"Fuck. Alright thanks man. Keep doing your thing. Let me know as soon as you have anything else. I don't care if it's concrete evidence or a damn rumor. I want to know everything." I tell him.

"You got it, Prez." He says as he rises from the chair before turning to walk out of my office.

I follow him as far as the hallway before heading in the opposite direction. Sliding onto a stool at the bar with a desperate need to wash the foul taste of this assholes story out of my mouth.

Surprisingly, Mac is already there. Not that it's unusual to see him at the clubhouse, but he normally has his fiancée glued to his side. It's not often he lets her out of his sight while they're here. Something about sticking close to reap the benefits of her voyeuristic tendencies.

"Hey, man. What are you doing here?" I ask as I settle on the stool next to him, signaling to the prospect behind the bar. I give him a nod of thanks when a glass of whiskey drops in front of me a minute later.

"Joker needed to talk to Kate about their project but he didn't want to leave Sarah, so we came here. They should be finishing up soon. I'm just the chauffeur today." He jokes.

I laugh, knowing damn well he is so far from *only* Kate's chauffeur.

"Brother, I hope you didn't say that shit to her. Your ass is gonna be sleeping on the couch." I laugh.

Demi would have no problem kicking my ass to the doghouse if some dumb shit like that came out of my mouth. As close as she and Kate are now, it wouldn't surprise me in the least if she put the idea in Kate's head.

"Naw, man." He laughs. "You think I'm stupid?"

Before I can say anything else, Sarah comes crashing in from the kitchen, Joker hot on her heels. A wide-eyed Kate follows a minute later, deer in the headlights look plastered all over her face as she sidles up to Mac.

"I said no, Joker! You don't get to tell me how to live my life!" Sarah is trembling with rage, and maybe a little bit of fear from the looks of it.

I don't even realize I'm on my feet until I'm stalking their direction. Not sure what they're arguing about but knowing the shit storm going on in the brother's head lately, I'm sure I can make an educated guess.

"Hey, Sarah. You good?" This situation needs to be de-escalated stat and not just because her kids are running around here.

The man looks ready to blow and that bullshit is the last thing Sarah needs to deal with. Not after everything she's already been through.

He would never hurt her or any woman for that matter but he's also never been in this situation before and it's messing with his head. I can't say he's handled it absolutely right, but he's giving it his best shot with no kind of instruction manual. Is he perfect? Hell, no. Nobody is.

"No, I'm not. You need to talk some sense into this idiot." The thumb she throws over her should leaves no doubt which idiot she's referring to.

My gaze shifts to the man at her back. He looks ready to explode, steam rising from his thunderous expression at her name calling.

"You got it. You go ahead and get back to the kids and I'll talk to him." Some of the rage leaves her expression as she gives me a short nod then takes off like a bat out of hell.

Once she clears the room, I turn a pointed look Joker's way. "Come on, man. Have a drink. You can tell us what dumbass edict you tried to lay on her."

Sitting back down, the prospect behind the bar doesn't wait for Joker to ask, sliding an entire bottle of whiskey in front of him, foregoing the glass.

Guess it's gonna be a long night.

"Do I even need to ask what you said to her?" I start.

Joker unlocks his jaw enough to answer me. "Fuck off, man."

"Let me guess. You did the exact thing I told you not to do? Demanded instead of asked? Told her she has to quit the bakery." Mac chimes in, Kate cozied up between his legs with humor lighting her face. "Or that you were putting her on lock down."

From the tightening of Joker's jaw, looks like Mac hit it right on the head. The wince on Kate's face confirming that is precisely what went down.

Honestly, I don't even know what to say. The brother was warned. Told time and time again to handle her with kid gloves and he was doing good for a while there.

"Fuck. This is my fault." Guilt eats at me. This entire clusterfuck with Demi's ex is causing all kinds of drama in the clubhouse.

"Naw, Prez." Mac denies. "You played your hand perfectly with your woman. It's this jackass that didn't play his cards right. That's not on you."

Well shit, he can never just leave it be. Always has to push Joker too far.

Stepping between them before they can come to blows again, I lay my hand on Joker's shoulder when he pushes himself off the bar to lunge at Mac. Not a care that his woman is sitting right there with him.

"Stop, Joker. Mac might be shit for explanations but he's right. You need to calm down and approach this from another angle." I tell him.

"What the fuck am I supposed to do now, Prez?" Rubbing a hand down his face, weariness is like a two-ton weight dropping on his shoulders. "She already said she's gonna leave. Start looking for a place for her and the kids. I can't lose them."

"The first thing you're gonna have to do is trust me, man. Trust me when I say we have them protected. Nothing is gonna happen to Sarah." I tell him for what feels like the millionth time.

We've talked this shit in circles and I'm about tired of it at this point.

"You know it's not about trust. I'd die if something happened to her, Lily or Joey." He mumbles around the mouth of the whiskey bottle.

"I know that brother, but does she?" I ask, "Does she understand what your real motive is or does she think you're just being a dick?"

His lack of response is answer enough. Before Sarah, Joker was the most even keeled brother among us. Since then, though, he's a powder keg waiting for a match to spark an explosion. Definitely not the best impression if he wants more from her.

He's coming from a good place though, and that is the only reason he's getting any kind of patience from me but if he doesn't pump the brakes, he's gonna push her too far. I'm afraid if that happens, Sarah will hightail it out of the clubhouse and out all our lives with a quickness.

"Prez has never steered us wrong, Joker. If he says he's got her covered, you gotta believe him. Otherwise, what the hell are you still doing in this club?"

Mac's words are harsh, but understandable when he's the one that's taken the brunt of Joker's rage lately.

"Fuck, you're right." Joker says. "I don't know what the fuck is going on with me. I ain't ever felt this way before."

No shit.

"And second and most important, brother, you need to fix that shit with your woman. I gotta say, I don't have a lot of faith in your ability to do that right now but I'm sure you'll figure it out."

And then I get the hell out of dodge before any more hell breaks loose.

I've got my own woman at home to figure shit out with.

Chapter Twenty-Nine

Demi

My bestie flounces through the door of Sweet Treats right on time. She's on a mission to unearth my secrets and is *so* not playing around.

I'm conflicted. On the one hand, I am damn proud of the self-confident woman in front of me after the bullshit of her upbringing. On the other hand, all that persistence focused on me? Not gonna lie, I'm not really a fan at all.

But I know when I'm beat, so I give the counter one more good swipe before heading to the kitchen to toss the towel on top of the full basket. Maybe I could sneak those up the stairs real quick and start a load of laundry. Anything to delay the inevitable, right?

Don't be a coward. It's not like you're facing a firing squad.

It sure does feel like it though.

Straightening my shoulders, I march my ass over to our table and drop down in the chair across from my bestie. Sarah must have been busy during my cowardly moment, two yummy caffeinated concoctions sit on the table between us.

And Sarah, bless her, is doing her best to look busy cleaning out the pastry case while casting surreptitious looks our way.

Girl sure could use some pointers on subterfuge.

"Sarah, get your butt over here and sit down. I might as well get this over with in one go. No need to have to repeat my stupidity any more than necessary." I call out.

Sarah's isn't the only head turning my direction. Danger and Bomber, my babysitters for the day, swing their attention my way too.

The brothers do nothing to hide their curiosity. Or should I say nosiness. Even though I know they already know my story, they're salivating at the mouth for all the deets since Ryker only gave them the Cliff Notes of my history before arriving in Frostown. These boys could rival the busy bodies down at the diner.

"Alright, hit me. What do you want to know?" I throw down the gauntlet.

My girls share a look before Kate blurts out. "Um. Everything, but first are you in danger?"

Leave it to my bestie to jump in feet first. She sure has grown some balls since the first time I met her.

I can't help the proud mama bear moment that hits me. Kate has come a long way since the timid mouse that first walked through my doors.

"Honestly, I don't know but Ryker seems to think so." I hedge.

Way to bury your head in the sand, girl.

"And this has something to do with your past? From before you came to Frostown?" Kate asks.

If I thought sharing my story with Ryker was hard, it's got nothing on confessing my shortcomings to my admirable bestie.

Emotions clog my throat, knowing how truly blessed I am to have her in my life and how deeply I ache for her approval. If I have to watch pity – or even worse disappointment – flash across her face, I really don't know how I'll survive the experience.

Blowing out a harsh breath, I give voice to the stupidity of my youth. "Yes, it's because of my past. I met my ex, Dwight, back in Sacramento. That's where I lived before I moved here. He was a member of another MC. One so completely different from the Broken Souls."

I trail off, memories assaulting me. The things I saw inside the walls of their club. The suspect behavior. The shady members. I was so stupid to turn a blind eye. Too afraid to ask questions.

"Demi?" Kate lays her hand over mine and I flip it palm up, latching onto the comfort and support I didn't even realize I needed to get this out.

"So, yeah. We were together for about six months. I didn't even realize what he was doing but in hindsight, it was classic abusive behavior. Cut me off from friends. Tried to cut my family out too but they wouldn't have it. I'll never be able to express how grateful I am that they never gave up on me."

"Did he hurt you?" The whispered question comes from Sarah, a look of shame crossing her face. Like she has firsthand knowledge of that shit.

"Yes, he did. One time. The day he hit me is the day I told him we were done and I moved in with my mom. Things were better for a while but then weird stuff started happening. The straw that broke the camel's back was when he broke into my home. Destroyed whatever he could get his hands on. Bastard called to gloat about the devastation he created."

Staring out the window, I wonder for the millionth time if leaning on the club is the best idea. If anything happened to Ryker, Kate or anyone else trying to keep me safe, I would never forgive myself.

That thought has circled my brain the last three days. A constant struggle to stop myself from running again. To keep them safe.

A squeeze to my hand brings me back to the moment. "Demi don't do anything stupid. I can see it written all over your face." A gentle smile softens her words. "Do you care about Ryker?"

"Yes." It's barely a whisper. A cautious admittance that I fear will bring my bad karma crashing down on him.

"Then you need to let him do what he does best. Ryker is their President for a reason. Each and every member of the club believes in him. They know the kind of man he is and he will protect you with his life." She sure knows how to make me feel like an asshole for even considering abandoning him.

"Don't you see? That's exactly what I'm afraid of, Kate. What if something happens to him because of me? If everyone loses the man they all care so much about because of my bullshit?" I admit my greatest fear.

"Do you honestly think they don't care about you the same way, Demi?" Surprisingly, the question comes from Sarah. "I know I haven't been around long, but what I can say is that man has been obsessed with you since the day they saved me and my kids from my husband."

Sarah's admittance takes me aback. I had a hunch she had it rough before coming to the MC, but for them to be the ones to save her? I had no idea.

"Are *you* okay, Sarah?" She seems like she has some demons of her own to exorcise.

Breaking eye contact, she glances around before answering in a low voice. "Most days, yes. Sometimes though I feel like Vinny will pop up out of nowhere and force me to go back. I'm afraid I won't be as strong as you if that day ever comes. I should have left a long time ago." Shame colors her words but my girl doesn't break eye contact.

Gripping her hand on the table, I look her square in the eye. "I don't ever want to hear you talk like that. I may not know all your story but what I do know is the amazingly kickass woman that you are. It doesn't matter how long you stayed. What matters is you survived. You took the first opportunity to get your babies out of a shitty situation."

"She's right, Sarah. You have nothing to be ashamed of. You *are* amazing and we were all ridiculously lucky the day the guys brought you and your kiddos into our lives." Kate adds.

I couldn't have said it better myself.

Just when I thought the spotlight was off me, Kate turns serious eyes my way. "And you. You need to talk to Ryker. Believe in him." Sternness echoes in her voice.

Guess what they say is true, you can take the teacher out of the school but you can't take the school out of the teacher.

"I couldn't live with myself if something happened to him." I admit. "Sometimes I wonder if it would be better for everyone, especially Ryker, if I gave myself over to Dwight."

"The fuck is that happening!" I about jump out of my seat as Ryker's booming voice echoes from the back of the bakery.

Oh shit.

"Uh oh. I think you might have pushed him too far this time." Kate stage whispers behind the hand that flew to her mouth at Ryker's outburst.

Way to state the obvious, bestie.

Chapter Thirty

Ryker

"Hey, man. Thanks for coming by." I offer my hand to the sheriff. We've been working close since starting the project for Kate's safe haven but this is his first trip to the clubhouse. The man has been a godsend, helping us cut through all the red tape for the project.

Elected in a landslide not long after we moved to Frostown, Zeke has treated us with nothing but respect in all our interactions. When Mac's woman was kidnapped, he stepped in to shut down any fallout from our not quite legal extraction.

It certainly helped that he served with Rocker in the Marines. The two fought side by side for years before he left the service. From what I understand, he worked as a detective on the intense streets of Chicago before moving to Frostown. Something about needing a change of pace from the bureaucracies of a big city.

Add in the fact he's the only man I've ever met to rival Rocker in the size department, it's no wonder the town took one look at his stellar record and intimidating presence and made him the new sheriff with a quickness.

"Nice to see you again, man." His grip is strong, eye contact steady before he swings around to check out the clubhouse. "Nice place you got here. Been meaning to come check it out sooner but the people in this town have kept me surprisingly busy."

"I wish this was a request for a social call but you're welcome to stop by anytime." I tell him.

"Rocker mentioned a possible issue. You got somewhere we can talk?" He scans the main room again. It's a quiet morning around here, most of the members out taking care of their own personal shit.

Leading him to the bar, I set my coffee down on the gleaming wood top. "We're good here. Everyone in the club knows most of what I'm gonna tell you."

"Okay. How worried do I need to be?" He settles on a stool, leaning tatted forearms on the bar.

"This is really just a heads up. We don't have anything concrete but there's a chance another club may try to move in on the town and let's just say they aren't anywhere near as friendly as we are."

I go on to give him the entirety of Demi's story, not leaving a single detail out. Give him the history on her ex's club activities too. The law in this town needs to be armed with all the intel if we're going to work together to head off the possible threat.

"I've got my tech guy digging into them but so far, there's no sign of them around town. That doesn't mean they aren't here. From what Byte found, they don't flaunt their colors when they start stirring shit up." I caution.

"Well, fuck. I gotta admit this isn't what I was hoping to deal with my first year here." Stroking the beard covering his jaw, he stares sightlessly at the array of liquor bottles on the shelves behind the bar.

He turns a pointed look my way before continuing. "I assume you had your guy try to trace this phone call?"

"I got nothing to hide, man. Are we toeing the line into the grey area? Fuck yeah. Do I give a shit what I have to do to keep my woman safe? Hell no." I tell him.

"I can respect that. I got my own guy. I'll have him look into it. From what Rocker said, he's probably not as good as yours but it doesn't hurt to put another set of eyes on this. Anything else I should know?" The more he talks, the more my respect grows.

"No, that's all we have at this point but I'll be sure to keep you updated. Appreciate you stopping by." The opening of the clubhouse doors grabs his attention right as I finish.

His jaw about drops to the floor as he catches sight of the ladies strutting in. Shockingly, it looks like they finished their little shopping excursion early. It's not unusual for the ladies to make an entire day of these trips. Retail therapy or some shit like that.

Laughter trails them as they cross the room, intent on the kitchen doors, arms laden down with grocery bags.

"Hey, Ryker! We finished up early but don't worry. We still about bought out the store!" Jade teases from the front of the pack.

"No worries. You need any help?" I ask.

"We're good. A couple of the guys are bringing in the rest. Thanks though." She may answer me but her eyes are all for the man at my side.

"We'll get out of your hair." She says as she eats him up.

Questions swirl in the Sheriff's own eyes when I turn back to him, but he holds them until the ladies clear the room.

"Who the fuck is that?" He demands, making no effort to hide his interest.

"Brother, pull your tongue back in your mouth." I laugh. "That's one woman I doubt you can handle. Sweetest girl you'll ever meet but she'll talk your damn ear off. Aside from her chatty nature, Jade likes variety in her men if you get my drift. Not sure you're up for that challenge."

I issue the warning seriously. Jade is one woman that will never be happy settling down with just one man.

"Hmm. I guess we'll just have to see about that." Interestingly, he doesn't seem put off by that piece of intel one damn bit.

"You know, I thought I'd run into Rocker today. I do have to say that was much better scenery than the big bastard." The man's got jokes. He might fit in around here just fine.

"I'll be sure to pass the message on to him." I say with my first genuine smile of the day.

Slapping me on the back, he rises to his full height, sauntering to the door just as the women exit the kitchen. Jade leading the charge as usual.

It's comical to watch every single one of them shut right the hell up as Zeke tips his cowboy hat in their direction. "Ladies. You have a great rest of your day."

Their jaws literally drop as he heads out the door.

I make my own escape as they swing to me in unison, the million questions rolling off their tongues falling on deaf ears.

I beeline straight to the bakery, my own woman back to the forefront of my mind. Not that she ever really leaves my thoughts but she's front and center once again as I ponder the situation.

Pulling up at the back of the bakery, I climb off my bike and enter through the backdoor.

From the feminine chatter up front, it sounds like Kate finally cornered my slippery woman.

I gotta say I admire her tenacity, succeeding where I failed with the damnable woman.

Employing an impressive arsenal of avoidance tactics, the woman snuck out like a thief in the night before I could get my hands on her this morning.

Instead of the conversation I fully expected to have, I woke to a note. Her scrawling handwriting cowardly explaining she caught a ride with the brothers on babysitting duty today.

"Kate, I couldn't live with myself if something happened to him. Sometimes I wonder if it would be better for everyone, especially Ryker, if I gave myself over to Dwight."

My good humor goes up in a cloud of smoke when the words falling from Demi's lips fully register.

"The fuck is that happening!" I roar.

This woman is gonna be the death of me.

Every head in the place swings my way as I stomp through the door.

"Ryker! What are you doing here?"

"What the fuck is wrong with you, woman? You honestly think I would let you give yourself over to that bastard?" Rage pounds through my veins at just the thought of her doing something so foolish.

She at least has the good sense to look chagrined at her harebrained idea but that doesn't stop her from pushing for more. "Just hear me out, Ryker. I've been thinking about it a lot. In fact, it's all I've been able to think about. We could set a trap for him. Get him out in the open to end this once and for all."

I'm already shaking my head. "Not a chance in hell, Firecracker. I will not allow you to put yourself in danger like that."

My heart races, blood pounds in my temples as I try to rein in my anger. This woman pushes all my damn buttons. The only person I have ever met foolish enough to push my control beyond all reason.

The legs of her chair scrape across the floor like fingers on a chalkboard as she stands from the table. Fearless in her indignation, she stalks around the counter, stepping right up to me until we're toe to toe.

Tiny little finger poking my chest, her breasts heave as the words fly from her mouth. "I don't think so, Big Guy. You don't dictate to me. I make my own decisions and if I think this is the best way to protect the man I love, then I'll damn well do it!"

Gasps sound from the peanut gallery but I only have eyes for the fiery temptress in front of me.

Putting her admission aside for the moment, I lean down until we're eye to eye. "You will not sacrifice yourself for me. You got it?"

And then I swoop in. Taking her completely by surprise, I cover her mouth with my own. Tongue invading, I feast on her. Slanting my head, I lick inside her mouth, thrusting and retreating as she challenges me for control.

Hands on her ass, I lift until her legs wrap around my waist, tempting and teasing until she's as lost in our kiss as I am. A clearing throat penetrates the sexual fog just enough to remind me other people are still in the room.

"Hey, Prez. Joker and Mac just pulled up. You want anything before we take off?" Rocker asks.

"Naw, man. Go ahead and take off but be sure to keep in touch with Zeke. He's putting out feelers for any shady characters showing up in town." The words are garbled since I can't seem to fully break the connection of Demi's lips to my own but he gets the gist of it.

"Got it. We'll, um, see you back at the clubhouse." He says as the bell over the door rings out from the force of their exit.

But it's all background noise, same as Mac and Joker escorting their women out along with the turn of the lock on the front door.

Refocusing on the woman in my arms, I give her a good long look. "I think we need to talk."

With her declaration ringing in my ears, I climb the stairs feeling ten feet tall and bullet proof.

I'm the king of the world, stealing away with my queen to the apartment above the bakery.

My need at a boiling point, there's not a chance in hell I'll survive the torture of the long drive home before I have her.

Chapter Thirty-One

Demi

Clinging to Ryker like a spider monkey, I hang on for the ride as he stomps his way up the stairs to my apartment above the bakery.

The staleness in the air is a startling contrast when he swings through the door of my abandoned home. Not that it really feels like home anymore. No, my home is the man I'm currently attached to and I'm woman enough to admit that to myself.

The smirk on his face as he sets me on my feet sets my spidey senses tingling. Gone is the anger from moments ago. In its a place is a fierce look full of possession.

Me thinks the Big Guy is up to something.

I won't lie, it scares me a bit. Not in a physical way or anything like that. No, this is a man on a mission and I'm not quite sure what his endgame is just yet.

"What are you up to, Big Guy?" Suspicion laces my words.

Might as well take the bull by the horns and all that.

That darn smirk grows as he moves right up into my personal space, face dropping down to meet me eye to eye.

"So, you love me, huh?" If that isn't a question full of smug satisfaction, I don't know what is.

"Hmm. Did I say that? I can't seem to remember." I put on an innocent expression.

One I've perfected over the years in the company of my mirror. I gotta admit that is definitely a challenge what with the devious ideas swirling around my head. My imagination runs wild with all the possible ways to wipe that sexy smirk right off his face. So many endless possibilities I don't even know where to begin.

"You damn well know you did, Firecracker." Never does he let me get away with my shit.

"Maybe I did. Maybe I didn't." I hold tight to the charade, taking two steps back to eye him up and down. My body still can't decide what to focus on first.

"Demi." God, that growl. It's ridiculously embarrassing how perfectly his rough voice hits me right in my girly parts.

Even if I live to be a hundred years old, that sexy growl will be just as potent as it is today. No doubt in my mind the effect he has on me won't dim one damn bit.

"What's wrong, Big Guy?" I purr, yanking my shirt over my head at the same time releasing my hair from the confines of its band. The loose tresses fall around my shoulders, sliding over my shoulders to play peek-a-boo with my breasts.

And all the while, Ryker watches, a captivated voyeur eagerly anticipating the coming show.

"What do you think you're doing, baby?" He asks but I'm a show more than tell kinda girl, so I run my hands down to the waistband of my pants.

Ryker doesn't stand idle. No, he slides his hand sensually down his stomach. Playing along, he wraps those strong fingers tight around his hardening cock behind the confines of his jeans.

The erotic action freezes all movement, I'm so completely caught up in the sight of this big man touching himself. Even through the material of his jeans the sexy show is the most delicious aphrodisiac.

I am spellbound by the performance he puts on just for me. Torturing his length, the muscles in his forearm rippling hypnotically as he loses himself to the hedonism of his actions.

"Keep going, Firecracker. I sure am enjoying the show." His order is gruff, knowing just how to work me. No doubt in his mind I'll follow his command.

My fingers fumble through the motions as I unbutton and oh so slowly draw down the zipper of my pants.

Two can play this game.

Slipping my thumbs in the material at my sides, I swivel my hips like a belly dancer as I shimmy them down my legs.

"Someone needs to catch up." I sass with a pointed look at the shirt hiding that impressive physique.

Gone with a quickness, he gives me an unobstructed view of his thick cock straining to escape his jeans.

"Come here, Firecracker." I follow his command like a puppet on a string.

Stepping directly in front of him, I do the unexpected, reaching for the button on his jeans at the same time I drop to my knees. A fiery desperation to see more of the show my only motivation.

With a shake in my hands, it takes me a minute to accomplish my goal. And throughout it all, Ryker continues to watch. Not lifting a damn finger to help, he keeps up the sweet torture.

With the mental fist pump of the century, I celebrate my victory when the material loosens enough to slide down his trim hips. My hands roam over thick tree trunk size thighs until his glorious cock springs free.

Standing tall and proud in front of me, Ryker is every bit the man with all the power as wraps his big hand around that beautiful cock. My reward is glorious as I finally get an unencumbered view of the show.

Those strong capable fingers pump his cock ever so slowly. Long torturous movements up and down until I don't think I can take any more. My mouth waters, eager to lay claim to his gorgeous appendage.

"This what you want?" He asks.

Is that a trick question?

He damn well knows that is exactly what I want.

Locking on those blazing emerald orbs, I do nothing to hide my enthusiasm. "You know I do."

"What are you gonna do with it?" He demands.

Unconsciously, my tongue slips out to lick my lips, mouth salivating at the thought of playing with him to my heart's content.

He might be huge but I'm up for the challenge. I'll work him so good he won't know what hit him when I've got him buried deep down my throat.

"I asked you a question, Firecracker."

Glancing back up, I admit my desire. "I want to put my mouth on it."

I'm burning up, my gaze unwittingly drawn back to the erotic sight in front of me. Mind unable to decide what to focus on as Ryker slows his strokes, hand squeezing the base of his cock to stave off his pleasure.

I squirm, searching for any kind of friction on my neglected clit. Anything to ease the ache in my core, my panties completely ruined at this point.

"Lean forward and open your mouth." I surprise us both, following his order like a good little girl as he moves his hand down until the head of his cock lines up perfectly with my open mouth.

The first touch of his flesh on my tongue quiets my mind, silences the static that's been on a constant loop for what seems like forever. The salty flavor that is all Ryker bursts on my tongue as I close my lips around him.

Eyes falling to half-mast he holds me captive, a willing slave shackling myself to the desire burning between us.

Suctioning my lips around his velvety length, I take him deeper. His pleasure my pleasure, I let my senses lead the way.

I am a woman on a mission. A mission to push him past the breaking point. A battle I'm fighting to win.

Do or die, there's no try in this bitch.

My body revels in the power I wield.

Why? Because a woman on her knees is the most powerful being in the world.

And don't let any fool tell you different.

"You're a greedy little thing, aren't you?" The words rumble through his chest, a vibration I feel all the way down to my core.

But that just won't do. If he can talk, I'm doing something wrong. So I double down with an eager nod, deviousness dancing through my blood. Upping the ante, I throw all my effort into bringing him to his knees. To give into the desire boiling right below the surface.

To use me.

In any way he wants.

And then it happens. He sinks his fingers in my hair, taking complete control of my movements. My desire at the precipice, moans roll up my chest, a hum of vibration up and down his length as he picks up his pace.

"So beautiful. On your knees for me."

My senses scatter to the wind when his pace turns frenzied, forcing the entirety of his length down my eager throat.

I'm not blind to the fact this is no regular occurrence for him, this man that never relinquishes any kind of control. The power of the exchange lights a fire in my core, taking me right to the precipice of my own orgasm.

"Demi." The rawness in his voice, a battle lost to the pleasure I'm delivering.

I double down on my efforts. Taking him as far as I can, swallowing around the swollen head of his cock. My hand moves in tandem, milking his cock just how he likes. Eyes locked on his face for the entirety of the ride.

My reward is sweet just short seconds later.

Literally.

This beautiful man roars his release, my name a silent prayer on his lips.

With smug satisfaction, I slip my hand in my panties. Fingers slipping and sliding, one touch to my clit sends me soaring through the stars.

And his eyes catch it all as I moan through my orgasm before giving him one last lingering lick and popping my mouth free.

With a touch so gentle, he slides his thumb over my lower lip at the same time his cock pops free. Gathering the release that escaped from my mouth before pushing his way in.

As I give that digit the same loving care, he leans down, hands slipping under my arms to lift me to my feet.

When he has me where he wants me, he presses a soft kiss to my lips before shocking the hell out of me. "I love you too, Firecracker."

A feather light kiss brushes my lips. "So, get that shit out of your head about giving yourself up for me. I will die before I let anything happen to you. Got it?"

Well shoot, he sure knows how to set a girl's panties on fire.

"Okay." The admittance is nothing but a whisper over his lips as they crash down on mine.

Chapter Thirty-Two

Demi

There is a party in full swing when we arrive at the clubhouse. Ryker sticks close, guiding me through the mass of people on the dance floor. His destination clearly the bar on the opposite side of the room.

What feels like an eternity later, we reach the bar at last to find Jade, Raquel, Dana and Danger in a loose circle around Mac where he sits in his usual spot at the bar. My bestie snuggled up nice and cozy in his lap.

In this unguarded moment, the look on his face as he leans down to hear what she has to say is pure worship. The chaste press of his lips to hers adorable in its sweetness.

I feel nothing but happiness for Kate and Mac, they went through a lot of shit, obstacles that would have demolished the connection between a lesser couple.

Moving in close, I pull her to me for a hug. Well as much as I can since Mac doesn't release his hold on her hips. We end up in sort of an awkward one-armed side hug I've seen the men around us do a hundred times. No less awkward than I always assumed it would be when I witnessed it.

"Demi! I missed you!" Jade pulls me away from my bestie to wrap her slim arms around me too. Her enthusiasm is contagious, a giggle falling from my lips at her antics.

While I may not be as close to Jade as I am Kate, she is quickly bulldozing her way into my pack. The woman thinks nothing of hiding her emotions. The absolute joy she takes in the little things in life a balm to my sarcastic soul. A lot like my bestie in so many ways. Only a little more blasé about her sex life. *Okay. A lot more.*

She lives life by the seat of her pants and makes no apologies for it. You don't like it? She'll throw you the middle finger and keep right on keeping on. I absolutely love that about her.

"How are you girls?" I ask the group as I'm passed around for more hugs hello. A grumbling Ryker must get tired of sharing because he yanks me back to his side before Danger can wrap his arms around me too.

"Looking good, Demi." With a smirk, Danger decides to play with fire. The wink he throws me right in Ryker's face proof he's aiming to get a rise out of his President.

"You too, Danger. Haven't seen you around lately. Where you been hiding out?" I play along.

"Here and there. Been helping my neighbor with some repairs out at her place." He says.

"Her, huh? You got an ulterior motive there buddy?" I can't help teasing.

A smirk edges his lips. "Wouldn't you like to know."

"It sure does get hot out there this time of year. I bet she's enjoying the show. All those muscles on display." I shoot him a wink of my own along with an exaggerated shiver, holding strong in the game for as long as I can.

The growl emanating from the man at my back tells me I'm playing hard ball here. Then again, when aren't I? I do so love to push his buttons.

With the winning play, Ryker yanks me impossibly closer, my backside dropping right into his lap as he sits down next to Mac.

Of course, it's absolutely where I want to be but I can't let on to that fact just yet. I let loose with a huff of indignation to mask my pleasure when his hardness slides deliciously against my backside.

I'm distracted from my victory as I catch sight of Byte crossing the room, heading right in our direction.

Uh oh. That's a pretty serious look on his face.

My suspicions are confirmed when he stops next to Ryker. "Prez, we got a problem." He says with a glance in my direction, making it clear whatever bad news he has is somehow related to my situation.

"What is it?" Ryker stiffens behind me.

"My guy keeping an eye on the Black Demon's reported half their members disappeared overnight. The club is a ghost town. The only thing left is a handful of members and the women they're holding there." Byte explains with another not-so-subtle look in my direction, probably to catch my reaction to the news.

"Wait. What women?" I ask as I start to stand but Ryker doesn't let me get far. Hands tightening on my hips, he keeps me locked down on his lap.

"We'll talk about it later." He tells me.

"What the hell, Ryker. Don't pull that shit with me. We'll talk about it right now." I demand as I yank myself away from him.

Thankfully, Jade is right there to catch me before I fall flat on my face. But I don't give a shit. I want answers and I want them right now.

That thought the only thing in my head, I spin to the man now glowering my way.

"What the hell is going on? Are they holding women there against their will?" My voice is shrill, cutting through half the conversations in the huge room as heads turn my direction.

Nothing new there.

Meeting my gaze head on, Ryker watches my reaction as he speaks. "Yes, they've got women they're holding there. Been doing it for years."

"And you didn't think to tell me this?" My voice could shatter some windows now.

"What do you think you can do, Demi? It's not like you can go in there and save them on your own." Damn him for being the voice of reason. That shit just pisses me off.

"Were any of them there when I was with Dwight." I ask.

From the tightening of his jaw, it's clear he doesn't want to answer me but that is just unacceptable. "Answer me, dammit."

"Yes. A couple of them have been there since you were there." He eventually admits.

"Fuck you, Ryker. How could you keep that from me?" The hurt that flashes through me just fuels my anger.

I can't even look at him right now. Turning away, I go to stomp away from the infuriating man but again he doesn't let me get far.

Arm snaking around my waist, he spins me to face him once more. Hand gently gripping my jaw, he forces me to look him in the eye.

"Demi, there is *nothing* you could have done for those women. What do you honestly think would have happened if you tried?" He doesn't leave it at just that either. "You think they wouldn't have done the same damn thing to you if you tried something foolish like helping them escape?"

And isn't that the crux of my anger? The fact I waltzed around that freakin' place ignorant to the evils hiding in plain sight.

"Baby, you might be the fiercest woman I've ever met and God knows I respect the hell out of you for that but there was nothing you could do for them." He promises me.

Tears well in my eyes, unable to tear my gaze from his. Letting all the emotions swirling through me shine through.

"I could have tried, Ryker." I whisper for his ears only, sick at the thought that I've been sitting here having a blast. Hell, the last year has been the best of my life. You know, aside from the fact I'm running from a psycho ex.

Eyes softening, he lifts his hand to gently cup my cheek. "Baby. Don't cry. I don't think I can handle your tears."

The gentle press of his lips to my forehead just makes the stupid tears fall freely down my cheeks.

I look up at him as he pulls back. "Ryker, we have to save them."

"We will, baby. You gotta trust me to handle it. The Sheriff is already working with his contacts out west. They will get them out of there but my priority is you. Making sure nothing happens to *you*."

With a shuddering inhale, I press my face to the comfort of his chest. A short nod my only response as the noise of the crowd goes back to normal now that the show is over.

Byte's voice cuts through the thoughts racing through my head. "By the way, Danger. I looked into the mechanic you asked me about. He's experienced. People have nothing but good things to say about him. I'd get him to check out your ride if I were you." He gives me a reassuring smile before walking away.

Bless him for taking the spotlight off my breakdown.

Chapter Thirty-Three

Demi

I wake to the sun streaming through the picture window in Ryker's bedroom. My body so deliciously sore from the marathon of orgasms the sexy man wrung from me last night. Even when I thought I had nothing left to give, he proved me wrong.

Multiple times.

And I am not mad about it.

Deciding to leave the sleeping beauty to rest, I slip silently from the bed before padding to the bathroom.

After washing my face and brushing my teeth, I head downstairs to start a much needed pot of coffee. I could mainline some caffeinated yumminess today.

Ryker has been insatiable the last two weeks and I am not complaining. Not one bit.

The things that man does to make me see stars is ridiculous. He's shown me a multitude of new positions, some I had no idea were even possible.

He pushes me just as much as I do him and I gotta admit the sex is off the charts because of it.

The ring of my phone is loud in the empty kitchen, echoing off the walls as I fumble to answer it before the noise carries upstairs to wake Ryker.

"Hello." I whisper the greeting without checking the caller ID.

"Hey, baby. It's good to hear your voice again." I shudder at the sadistic tone echoing through the line. One that I will unfortunately never forget.

"What do you want?" Anger fires my blood at the audacity of this asshole.

"You know what I want, sweetheart." The endearment sickens me but his next words chill my blood. "If you don't want something happening to the curly haired cutie, you'll do exactly what I say."

Fuck, how the hell does Dwight know about Kate?

"You've been watching me? How cowardly. You're not even man enough to show yourself. To come after me directly?" I demand.

"You know I can't do that. That guard dog you've attached yourself to won't ever allow me to get too close." Guess he's not as dumb as he looks. There is absolutely no way Ryker would let that shit happen.

And that thought there scares the shit out of me. I can't let Ryker pay the price for my bad decisions. I could never live with myself if something happened to him.

No matter my promise to let him handle this. To trust him to handle this, when it comes down it the risk is too great.

I can't take the chance, so with a resigned sigh, I make a fateful decision. One I'm sure will end badly for me no matter what happens. "Where do you want me to meet you?"

"I knew you couldn't wait to come home, *baby*." I shudder at the lust lacing that one word, the exact opposite of the pleasure Ryker ignites when he uses the endearment.

"Just get to the point, Dwight. Where am I going?" It's a good thing Ryker had my car delivered to the house last week. I'm sure he never considered that decision would give me the opportunity to break my promise to him. If he had any idea at all, he would have burned my car to a crisp before letting me get away.

Guilt starts to eat away at the fear in my head but Dwight's next words shut that down real quick. "Don't go doing anything stupid, bitch. If you try to set me up, it won't just be the pretty brunette that suffers."

Chills race down my spine at the threat in his voice, no doubt in my mind he will have no problem following through on that dark promise. Not after what I've learned about him and his club over the last few weeks.

"Relax, asshole. I said I'll be there. Now tell me where I'm going or I'm hanging up." I threaten, knowing how to push his buttons. But there's no joy in that knowledge.

"Get on the road to Redford. I'll call you once you're on the move and let you know where you're going." Smugness coats his words. And why wouldn't he be? The bastard is getting exactly what he wants.

I can't let myself go there right now or I'll lose my nerve. The only thing that matters is keeping Kate and Ryker safe.

His sadistic laugh cuts off abruptly as he hangs up the phone. Wasting no time, I rush to the door leading to the garage, snatching up my keys before jumping in my car.

All the while, praying to God Ryker doesn't come charging through the door.

As I start the engine, my mind races. The adrenaline pumping through my veins making it impossible to make heads or tails of my thoughts.

For every mile of distance I put between Ryker and myself, my doubt grows tenfold. But then a thought pierces through the chaos.

What the hell am I doing?

I slow down, my grip on the steering wheel tightening. The realization hits me like a ton of bricks. And when it does, I realize what a fool I am to even consider doing this.

I would rather face Ryker's wrath than play into this bastard's hands.

I *trust* Ryker. Trust him implicitly to eliminate this threat against us.

Like a sitting duck on the side of the road in the middle of nowhere, I bang my head on the steering wheel.

So, what the hell are you doing, girl?

I'll admit that's a damn good question. Even if I'm just talking to my damn self.

Chapter Thirty-Four

Ryker

Stirring from the best night of sleep I have had in years, my eyes flutter open then immediately snap back closed when I'm hit like a jab to the face by the sunlight invading my room. Should have closed the damn blinds last night.

Even with the bright rays of sun lighting up my bedroom, I reach for the comforting warmth of my woman with a smile full of eager anticipation.

We've had more sex in the last two weeks than I have in the last two years, unable to keep our hands off each other for more than five damn minutes most days.

Intent on delivering a wakeup call the sexy woman will never forget, my smile turns down when the only thing I encounter is the coldness emanating from the spot where Demi's tight little body should be. All remnants of a restful night's sleep wash away in a flash.

"Demi?" Voice thick with sleep, I clear my throat, trying again when I'm greeted with nothing but silence. "Demi!"

Worry gnaws at me when there's still no response.

Bolting upright in the bed, I let the covers fall away as I swing my legs over the edge, leaning down to grab my sweats from the floor where I dropped them haphazardly last night. A sense of foreboding filling me when the house remains eerily silent as I pull them on.

The usual sounds of Demi's coffee scented early morning routine conspicuously absent and let me tell you – you do not want to get between that woman and her caffeine addiction. I tried that once and learned my lesson with a quickness. Almost lost some fingers because of it.

My mind races as I do my best to push down my fear. Try to convince myself nothing nefarious could possibly have happened without my knowledge.

Snatching my phone from the nightstand, it rings as soon as I have it in hand. The sight of Byte's name flashing on the screen sends chills skittering down my spine. There's a tremble in my thumb as I press the button to put him on speakerphone.

"Demi's gone. What the fuck is happening?" I skip the pleasantries, pacing the room. Mind a whirlwind of fear and worst-case scenarios. A gut feeling some shit went down while I slept away, oblivious to it all like a dumbass.

Seconds feel like hours, each one an eternity as I listen to Byte do what he does best. Fingers like lightning, I listen to them fly over the keys of his laptop. My patience is thin, an urgent need to put eyes on my woman before something terrible can happen to her.

"Demi got another call from a blocked number. I didn't have time to trace it but she took off like a bat out of hell as soon as she hung up." Byte gets right to the point. "Tracker has her stopped on the highway to Redford."

There is not an ounce of guilt in my soul for invading her privacy and having Byte track her phone. It was a necessary evil. One I hoped like hell wouldn't be needed but is definitely coming in handy at the moment.

My hand itches with the need to teach her a lesson. Tie her to the bed she left me in until she admits her mistake. To show her what happens when she doesn't have faith in me.

You can bet your ass, as soon as I find her safe and sound – because really any other outcome is not an option – the infuriating woman won't be able to sit for a week when I'm done with her.

"I've got a location." Byte's voice pulls me out of the dark fantasy in my head. "She's not far from you. I'll send you the coordinates. You should wait for the brothers, Prez. You might need back up. "

My heart about pounds out of my chest as I race down the stairs. Foregoing my jacket, I grab my keys and explode through the garage.

"I need to get to her ASAP. Tell them to get their asses moving." I order. "I'm not waiting around."

No time to waste, I roar out of the garage, skidding over the dirt road then accelerating onto the highway at the end of my driveway. A roar of engines signals the brothers are busting their asses to catch up but my need won't allow me to waste a second to wait.

Flying down the two-lane highway, my thoughts race as fast as the miles passing under the wheels of my motorcycle. Every scenario worse than the last as I imagine Demi in the hands of that sadistic bastard. My mind spirals into the depths of despair with each minute that passes.

What feels like an eternity later, a single car comes into view not far up ahead. Pushing the throttle to the max, I roll up on the idling vehicle. Relief wars with anger when I recognize Demi's blond head whipping right to me at the sound of my bike.

I'm so pissed I can't see straight. Red haze lurks in my vision as I roll to a stop right next to her car. A million worst case scenarios rolling through my head, scenes from a horror movie screaming behind my eyes like a highlight reel of bad intentions.

But it's all for naught as the damn woman climbs from her car seemingly unharmed. I stalk to her, my anger at a boiling point. More pissed than I have ever been in my life.

I'm second guessing my desire for such a strong woman until she turns wary eyes my way.

"Ryker! What are you doing?" Her words carry a shit ton of optimism.

Cautiously optimistic, she approaches me like a wounded animal. Probably the smartest decision she's made all day.

That optimism slows my roll enough to calm the beast raging inside just enough for a sliver of reason to return.

She may be infuriating. She may not always think before she acts. But for better or worse, this woman is mine and it's about time she admits that truth. I stalk her like prey, backing her all the way up until she's flattened between the car and my body.

"You're mine Demi. God knows, I've given you the time you need to come to terms with that but I'm done waiting. I take offense when another man thinks he has any right to call you his. To think he can take you away from me."

I press my lips gently to hers, conveying the conviction of my feelings. This kiss different than any other we've shared. I pour my heart into it. Doing with action what she's not picking up with words.

This woman owns me and she doesn't even know it. She doubts her self-worth. Thinks she's not worthy of love from a good man. I'm no saint but I'll treat her like a queen.

My Queen.

She'll never doubt herself again when I'm done with her.

Prying myself away takes all my self-control but I need to know she gets me.

"Do you understand me yet?"

Chapter Thirty-Five

Demi

Surrounded on all sides, the men of the MC form a protective barrier between me and any possible threat as we navigate the roads back to the clubhouse.

Before I even put the gear in park, Ryker is there in a flash, yanking the handle to fling the door open.

"Let's go." His voice is harsh. The man is still pissed as hell.

A little voice tells me I may have pushed him too far this time.

You think?

Where the hell was this voice of reason earlier?

A snort passes my lips at my internal dialogue, earning me another glare from the towering giant. As pissed as he is, still he surrounds me, a barrier of protection enveloping me in a bubble of potent masculinity.

Even in his anger, he's never been more beautiful. Never more arousing than in this moment.

This is exactly what I wanted, to see the beast inside unleashed. I just wish it wasn't my stupidity that pushed him past the breaking point.

"Ryker." I start to try to tame the beast but he cuts me off with a shake of his head, hand on my arm tightening just this side of pain. A firm warning of caution to keep my trap shut.

"Not now, Demi. Or so help me God, you're gonna find out what happens when you push me too far." His big body vibrates with the anger boiling his blood.

A shiver rocks my entire body. But not one borne of fear. No, this man would never hurt me. But the thought of him taking all that anger out in a different way? Showing me exactly what he can do with all that unleashed power. My lady parts are on fire.

So inappropriate, girl.

Leading me directly to his office, the air is still as every member of the club watches him frog march me like a convict to the gallows. Silence blankets the room as all eyes stay locked on the scene, powerless to look away.

I am officially screwed when the door slams behind us, cloaking us in the privacy he needs to unleash the beast.

Hand in my hair, he tightens his grip to the biting edge of pleasure. Twisting his hand, he takes his time. Oh, so slowly, wrapping the long strands of my hair around his fist until he grips the back of my skull. Pulling me back, he zeroes in on the sensitive column of my neck before leaning down to take a bite of the flexing tendons.

What he intended as punishment quickly turns to desire. As soon as this man lays hands on me I fall to pieces, reveling in the sensations only he has the ability to bring to life.

Even with the anger rolling off him in waves, the smoke pouring out his ears, I turn to mush. A puddle of desire ready to bow at his feet and do his bidding. No matter the ask.

"Look at me, Demi."

I didn't even realize my eyelids feathered closed until the growled demand passes his lips. With the effort of the century, I slide them open, immediately locked on that demanding gaze.

"I get that you've been doing this on your own for so long, but baby, you have to trust me." His words are like a punch to the gut.

The hopelessness that overwhelmed me in that fateful moment. The fear of losing him. It all boils over to explode out of my mouth. My deepest fears revealed.

"I thought I could, Ryker, but when Dwight called. When he threatened you. Threatened Kate." I swallow past the lump in my throat before I can continue. "I didn't think. There was absolutely no consideration of what could happen to me. All I could see was you or Kate hurt because of me. That just isn't a fate I could survive." I finish in a desperate whisper.

His green eyes sear down into mine. So serious it becomes impossible to look away. "I know, baby. Did you stop to consider what would happen if that sadistic bastard got his filthy hands on you? You really think I would have just let you go?"

Logically, I know that would never happen. Ryker would *never* just let me go. I was stupid to think that was ever a possibility.

This man would fight to the ends of the earth and beyond – destroy anything in his path – to save the one's he loves.

The truth is logic had no place in my decision making this morning. With a threat to his life, I reacted on pure instinct.

"No, I know you wouldn't and that's why I snuck out." I admit my cowardice.

"Demi, do you want to be with me? Really want it?" He asks as his fingers loosen in my hair, hand moving around to cup my cheek, thumb a distraction as it brushes back and forth.

"Yes." My voice is barely a whisper.

"Then this shit stops now. You have to trust me or I walk away. I'll still protect you because I just can't turn that off but if there's no trust, there is no *us.*" Leave it to Ryker to get right to the heart of things.

And isn't that a kick to the lady parts. As loathe as I am to admit my mistake, I know he's right. If I want this to work, I have to give this entire situation over to him to handle. No matter my fear, I have to let him take the lead on this.

"Okay." I whisper.

"I mean it, Demi." Sternness coats his words. A seriousness like I've never heard from him before. "You cannot pull some shit like this again. Do you understand me?"

Voice unwavering with the strength of my conviction, I give him what he wants.

No, what he *needs*. What we both need.

"Yes, Ryker. I understand."

Seemingly satisfied, he wraps his arms around me, pulling me close and hanging on tight. I breathe him in, taking in a lungful of Ryker scented air. A true sense of peace settling over me.

"Prez! We got a problem out here." Danger's voice intrudes from the other side of the door.

"Fuck. Hang on." He yells back. "I'll be out in a minute."

So much for privacy. Although it may not be such a bad thing. Emotions are raw. For the both of us. Probably a good time for a breather.

Ryker drops his forehead to mine, those fierce green eyes narrowing right in on mine. "We do this together, Firecracker. Side by side, okay?"

"I can work with that." He's offering exactly what I need. A man to fight with. Shoulder to shoulder on the battlefield of life. Whatever the future brings us.

A fist bangs on the door. "Seriously, Prez. You gotta get out here. Demi too!" Danger yells through the door once again.

"Come on, baby." A soft kiss whispers over my forehead before he pulls away from me.

Linking his hand with mine, out the door we walk. "Let's go see what we need to deal with. Together."

Side by side. Not in front of or behind me. This man treats me as his equal and it's about time I start doing the same.

Chapter Thirty-Six

Demi

All eyes are once again upon us as, hand in hand, Ryker and I return to the main room of the clubhouse.

The smile I couldn't control if my life depended on it falls flat when I see the dark-haired pixie standing toe to toe with the club's enforcer. A ferociousness I've never seen lighting up the face of my baby sister.

That's when all my good feels go up in a cloud of smoke.

"Amy? How the hell did you find me *here?*" I ask when she doesn't look away from the brute in front of her.

In fact, both of them ignore every single person in the room, locked in a battle of wills I'm really not sure I like.

"Rocker, back the hell away from my sister." My voice is steel. No one tries to intimidate my sister and lives to tell the tale. I give him my best death glare but the big asshole just ignores me.

I shouldn't have worried though. My baby sister holds her own with the big dude as their battle of wills continues. A silent communication I would give anything to hear given voice to.

It takes a minute before she finally tears herself away from the staring contest they're locked in. Then she's a flash of movement, barreling towards me with no signs of stopping until she has me wrapped up in a bear hug.

"Demi! I missed you." Her words are muffled by the mass of hair hanging loose around my shoulders as I fight to keep us both upright.

"Amy. You shouldn't be here." I may say the words but I wrap her up and hug her just as fiercely. Until this moment – until my sister was standing right here in front of me – I didn't realize how much I ached for my family.

"This is exactly where I need to be, Sis." She pulls back and gives me her best stern look. "You can't fool me, Demi. You've been distant since you came back here. More so even than before everything happened with Mom. Something is going on and I want to know what it is. I assume this has something to do with your douchebag ex?"

Well damn. Leave it to my too perceptive baby sister to figure it all out.

When did she get all grown up and shit?

Embarrassed at the mention of my ex and the unspoken reference to all my bad decisions, I take a quick glance around the room. Only to confirm that, yep, all eyes are *still* on me.

Thankfully, Ryker senses my discomfort, stepping forward with his hand extended to Amy.

The man is ridiculously attuned to all my emotions.

"I'm Ryker. Your sister's man. And yes, he found her here after she went home to see you all."

As expected, all color drains from my sister's face with that last little tidbit of info.

Dammit, he could have kept that part to himself.

"We're doing everything in our power to find him." He tries to reassure her when she goes deathly pale right in front of his eyes.

Thank God for Jade who steps up to distract her, taking the lead and introducing Amy to all the members gathered here tonight.

As soon as she hears Kate's name, my sister leaps forward and treats her to the same bear hug I received, strangling the life out of my friend who looks at me helplessly. I give her a shrug, my sister is on a mission to show her appreciation and there's not a damn thing I can do to stop her.

"I've heard so much about you! Demi couldn't stop talking about you when she came home. Words cannot express how grateful I am that my sister found you." She says as she pulls back to give my friend some much needed room to breathe.

She doesn't let her get far though, hooking her arm around my bestie's shoulders, she keeps her glued to her side. "She probably hasn't said it, so I'll say it myself. You've been a godsend for her."

"She's been the same for me. I couldn't imagine life without her. She keeps us all on our toes." Kate says with a wink thrown my way.

That comment gets a burst of laughter from Amy. "Yeah, I just bet she does. She definitely likes to stir some shit up. The things she used to talk me into. Life is definitely not boring with my sister around."

"Okay, okay. That's about enough from you two or I'm gonna have to separate you." And I'm only half joking. These two sharing stories has disaster written all over it.

The last thing I need is for the people of the MC to hear all the dumbass schemes I got up to in my youth. They'd never let me live that shit down.

"Sorry to interrupt. I really need to use the little girl's room. Anyone want to show me the way?" Amy asks.

Jade, the gem that she is, offers to show Amy the way. "Of course. Come with me."

As soon as they clear the room, I turn stern eyes on Rocker. Taking a page out of my bestie's book, I give him my best stern teacher glare.

"Do you like your balls, Rocker?" I ask the intimidating man but he doesn't take the bait, so I double down when all I get is a blank stare back. "You keep your hands to yourself if you want to keep them attached to your body."

Mama bear is in full effect right now, but the damn man doesn't even blink.

"She stays here." He says instead, ignoring my threat of bodily harm entirely.

"Like hell is that happening, buddy." I move to get right up in his face but Ryker snatches me around the waist, pulling me right back to his side before I can inflict bodily harm.

What? I took self-defense classes.

Okay, so maybe I only took one or two beginner classes. That doesn't mean I don't know things. I can still do some damage. Just ask Ryker. He's been on the receiving end of my deadly aim a time or two.

"He's right, Firecracker. This is the safest place for her right now. That way I don't have to split my focus between the two of you." Damn the man for being the voice of reason here.

Giving Rocker the stink eye, I issue another warning right as my sister and Jade clear the hallway. "I'll have eyes on you, buddy. Don't go trying to pull some shit with my baby sister."

I go to give him the universal "I've got my eye on you" sign but my sister grabs my fingers before I can throw them his way.

"Oh my God. Demi stop!" Color tinges her cheeks as she shoots a shy glance Rocker's way before her eyes skitter away.

Not sure what she's embarrassed about. She knows how I roll and that's right on the train to crazy town if anyone messes with my family.

"Amy. Why don't we get you set up in a room and I'll have your sister back here tomorrow morning." Ryker takes charge as usual.

"That's a hard pass for me if you're taking her to the bakery." She says. "The jet lag is real when you come from the west coast. Can someone give me a ride there when I get up?"

Jade laughs at my sister's outrageousness.

What can I say? It's au naturale for the Carter clan.

Linking arms with Amy, Jade steers her back to the hallway. "I assume you want to put her in your room, Ryker?"

"Yeah. Put her in there and we'll figure out what's gonna happen tomorrow." He tells her before turning back to my sister. "It was nice to finally meet you, Amy. Let anyone in the clubhouse know when you're ready to come out to the bakery and we'll make it happen."

"Got it." Jade tells him before leading my sister away.

Chasing after the ladies, I wrap my sister up in one more hug. "I missed ya, Sis." I whisper for her ears only. "I'll see you in the morning. And try to stay out of trouble, okay?"

Chapter Thirty-Seven

Demi

"So, what's the story on the big, bald hottie?" My devious sister asks where she leans a hip against the counter, her brows doing a ridiculous dance across her forehead. "Is he single? Ready to mingle?"

Unfortunately for my girl Sarah, her ill-timed drink of caffeinated deliciousness projects right back out her mouth from the outrageousness of my sister's question.

"Oh my God. Tell me you aren't exactly like her." The blurted words take us all by surprise. Sarah most of all, who slaps a hand over her mouth as her cheeks flame fire engine red. "I'm so sorry. I didn't mean that the way it sounded."

The bubble of laughter floating past my lips feels oh so good after the stress of the last month.

"Relax, girl. No offense taken." I assure my friend while handing her some napkins. "Believe me, I've heard much worse. There's not much that will offend me at this point in my life."

"And you." I shake my finger at my unruly sister, feeling a lot like a mama scolding a precocious child. "Behave. Don't go acting like a cougar on the prowl. You came to check on your favorite sister, remember?"

Waving me off, Amy has her mind set on a reconnaissance mission and will not be denied. "Whatever. I'm not *that* transparent. So, tell me all about him."

Poor Sarah has no idea the shenanigans she's embroiled herself in by coming into work today.

With an exaggerated sigh, I give my table of babysitters a surreptitious glance before giving my sister just enough to wet her thirst. "He served in the military with some of the brothers. I don't know which ones so don't ask.

181

He's intimidating as hell. Has to be to be the club's enforcer. Other than that, there's not much else I can tell you. The man is quiet as hell. Doesn't do a whole lotta talking."

"Hmm. Methinks you know more than you're letting on, Sis." Her eyes narrow in on my face. An attempt to read my innermost thoughts.

Someone should probably tell her mindreading isn't actually a thing.

"Besides it's not really talk I'm after if ya know what I mean." She says.

"So anyway. How long are you planning on staying?" I'm not touching that comment with a ten-foot pole, so I change the subject and I'm not gonna apologize for it. Anything to distract my sister from the scary ass brother.

"Not sure. Mom's doing better and Bianca let her lease go. So, she's living with her for the foreseeable future. The house has been a little too cramped if you know what I mean. There's only so many backhanded compliments I can take from sister dear."

From the finger quotes wrapping up the word compliments, seems like Bianca has switched targets since the easy one left the building. AKA me.

"She's pulling that crap with you now? I thought you two were getting along since I moved here?" I ask.

"You know Bianca. She's not happy unless everyone else is unhappy." Amy shrugs away my concern.

Eyes roaming the room, she switches topics so fast poor Sarah looks like she's getting whiplash. Unfortunately for her, it's a regular occurrence around here.

"This is a nice place you got here. You know I'm proud of you, right? Mom too. Making all your dreams come true. Even though you moved clear across the country to do it."

And cue the waterworks. Damn Amy for making me emotional.

That sure would give the busy bodies at the diner plenty of fodder for the gossip mill.

But it means so much to hear her say the words.

"You want a job?" I ask jokingly. Grasping at straws to head off the emotional breakdown barreling down on me like a freight train.

"That might not be a bad idea." She surprises me. I was not at all expecting her to want to stick around this town.

My hand freezes where I'm wiping down the display case as I turn to study her. "Really? Just how long are you planning on sticking around, Sis?"

I figured she'd be on the next plane back to California after witnessing the clear lack of entertainment we have going on around here. Things are not hopping in Frostown, that's for sure.

It's not that I don't *want* my sister to stay but what with my douchebag ex lurking in the shadows, I'm not so sure it's a good idea.

"Not sure. I can work from anywhere, so I thought I'd hang around a while. Help you out if you need it." The nonchalance she attempts to infuse in her words is not lost on me.

"What's going on, Amy?" I ask the question casually to mask my concern. With my sister, I have to tread delicately or she'll clam up with a quickness.

Now that I really look at her, I realize Amy has lost weight. Quite a bit actually since I last saw her a few weeks ago.

"There's nothing going on, Demi." She denies. "I really just missed you. Like I said Bianca is handling everything with Mom so I thought it would be a perfect time to check up on you."

Well damn. Now I feel like an asshole.

"You know I missed you too. You can't even imagine how hard this last year has been to not be able to just jump in the car to go see you." I tell her honestly.

"So does that mean I can stay?" There is no way I can deny her anything with all the hope rolling off her in waves.

"Let me talk to Ryker. If he thinks they can keep you safe indefinitely then I would love to have you stay." I agree.

A brilliant smile lights up her face at my compromise but then the little shit has to go and ruin our moment of bonding.

"So, your man, huh? Tell me all about him. Is he *big* all over?" She asks, eyebrows once again twerking across her forehead.

Ridiculous.

But she gets what she deserves when a spray of coffee hits her square in the face courtesy of my girl Sarah.

I can honestly say I don't feel bad, not one little bit for the brat.

Chapter Thirty-Eight

Demi

The motorcycle glides over the mountain road like a knife through butter as Ryker finally takes me on the ride he's been promising me all week.

The man has been on the move for days and I know he needs this little escape as much as I do. He's barely stopped to collapse into bed at night, surviving on an hour or two of sleep when his body gives out on him.

All too soon, he pulls over in a small clearing hidden up high in the mountains, close to the neighboring town of Thunder Ridge Falls. Although with a population of four hundred, it sure is a stretch to even call it that.

The view is magnificent as we take it in in companionable silence, neither one of us interested in dismounting the bike. It's no wonder the residents of this little lakeside community do their best to keep outsiders at bay.

At least that's the rumor that runs through the Frostown mills. I haven't made the trek into the sleepy little town yet so I can't say for sure.

When the silence continues for longer than I can stand, I lean forward to rest my chin on that broad shoulder of his.

"Whatcha thinking about so hard there, Big Guy?" Turning my face to his, I press a lingering kiss to his cheek to tempt his focus my way.

The view is beautiful and all but when he's got a willing woman at his back, I'm pretty sure there are better things to occupy his mind.

"Are you happy, Firecracker?" The question hits me out of left field. I'm not really sure where he's going with this line of questioning.

"Of course. What don't I have to be happy about?" Even the shit going on with Dwight doesn't hold a candle to the happiness this man has delivered since I got my head out of my ass and gave us a chance. "Where's this coming from?"

"I want you to move in with me." He says quietly.

"I'm already living with you, Big Guy." I tell him but he's already shaking his head.

Giving me his eyes for the first time since we rolled to a stop, the intensity – the *love* – shining back at me takes my breath away.

And then he rocks my world completely off its axis. "Permanently, baby. Not just because of the shit going on right now. I want you there with me way beyond that. Forever if I can lock you down that long."

Oh wow.

I swear panties burst into flames all over the world, swoons from women of all ages thunderous in the background. And let me tell you, they aren't the only ones.

My heart about beats out of my chest. Breathing is overrated.

I am so entirely blown away by the fact this man wants more with *me*.

But I have to be sure.

I am a handful. I'm woman enough to admit it and I am scared. So damn afraid he'll tire of my antics. Of my constant need to test him. To push his boundaries. To see just how quickly I can make him lose control.

"Are you sure?" All my insecurities ring through those three little words. The insecurities I hide behind a boatload of attitude.

"You got any more harebrained ideas about walking into another MC?" I'm already shaking my head before he even finishes the question.

That's a hard pass if I ever heard one.

"You looking to hook up with another man?" The question is delivered with a stern look like this is a test or some shit.

"Not sure I could juggle another man right now." I tease but he doesn't laugh so I cup his jaw and get serious.

"Why the hell would I do that, Big Guy? You're all the man I need."

He must like that response a whole hell of a lot better if the smirk tilting his lips is anything to go by.

"Do you honestly think there's anything you can do to surprise me at this point, Firecracker?"

"Maybe? You know I gotta keep you on your toes." I sass him just because.

That earns me a full-blown belly laugh. "Ain't that the truth."

I'll fully admit that sight leaves me a little bit stupid. The man is heart stopping when the stoicism drops. When he lets a tiny bit of that control slip.

The fact I'm the only one he drops the mask with? You bet your ass I'd fist bump my own damn self if I wouldn't look like an idiot.

The humor wipes away, leaving a tender look in its place. Eyes full of love, he tucks a strand of hair gently behind my ear. "Baby, I'm serious. I am so hopelessly in love with you. There's not a damn thing you could do that will change the way I feel about you."

Be still my heart. I am officially a puddle of goo at his feet.

"I want it all with you, Demi. The good, the bad and the ugly." He says with a soft smile. "And I think you do too."

I nod like an eager little thing. "I do, Ryker."

"Then say yes, Firecracker."

"Okay. Yes." Then I fling my arms around his neck and let him kiss the hell out of me, butterflies taking flight at the desire he stirs to life without fail.

Things escalate quickly after that. Before I know it, he's worked my jeans down my legs. Bent over the seat of his bike, my panties stretched to the breaking point where he left them around my thighs, I don't have much room to maneuver.

Something tells me he likes me just as I am. Absolutely at his mercy, no avenue for escape. What he doesn't know is I am right where I want to be.

I think I'll keep that little secret to myself.

I'm sure I look a sight. Pants down, ass up. Hanging over the seat of this big black beast. I am a quivering mass of need anxiously awaiting this sexy man's next move.

I about jump out of my skin when his big hand slides over the curve of my ass, giving it a nice hard smack for good measure.

Moans fall past my lips from the pleasure of that little love tap.

"So pretty offering yourself up to me like a wet dream, baby." I can't help but push my ass a little harder into his palm, seeking the pleasure this man delivers without fail. Every. Single. Time.

It's as if he's somehow snuck in and programmed my body to his every touch. Nipples bead. Cream escapes. Gasps fall freely as soon as he lays a finger on me.

And he's not done yet, going down on his knees, gripping my hips in those huge strong hands. He lifts me up just enough to slide beneath me.

"I promised you pleasure. Come sit on my face, baby." Not that he gives me much of a choice. Those big hands take a cheek in each palm and pull me right down where he wants me.

I scramble for purchase, digging my fingers into anything I can get my hands on. Knocking the bike on its side would really kill the mood right about now.

As soon as my pussy settles over his face, he does as promised. He *feasts* on me. Tongue lapping. Teeth nipping.

He drives me to the point of no return in seconds flat and I am just along for the ride, my hands tangled in his hair in an attempt to stay grounded.

Hips circling, I grind my pussy all over his gorgeous face. Mindlessly chasing my orgasm with not an ounce of shame.

The sight of this big bad leader of men on his knees just for me pushes me right to the precipice.

"Oh God. Yes, right there." Incoherent demands tumble past my lips.

He eats me with abandon. The grunts of his approval driving me higher. Riding the line between pleasure and pain, he nips my sensitive flesh before thrusting his tongue inside me. That oh so talented appendage hitting just the right spot. Fucking my pussy the way I want his cock to fill me right up.

"Come for me, Demi." He growls.

That demand is all it takes to send me soaring straight to the stars, his name a prayer on my lips.

Before I even float back to reality, Ryker is there, poised at my entrance. With one hard thrust, he buries his cock completely. The muscles of my core pulsing around him, sucking him in like a greedy little bitch.

He lasts through five more thrusts before burying himself deep and groaning his release into my neck. Teeth sinking in, a love bite taken in the heat of the moment.

I'm blanketed in a cocoon of tranquility as he collapses on top of me. Crushed firmly between his big body and the solid steel of his bike, I lose all the breath in my lungs.

Who needs air, right?

I am *exactly* where I want to be.

Chapter Thirty-Nine

Ryker

"The Demon's President was seen out in Redford and you're not gonna like who he was meeting with." Byte drops that bomb with a glance Joker's way before he turns back to me.

Shit. This can't be good.

A small group of us hauled ass to the clubhouse at Byte's summons, no questions asked. All the brother said was he had something big and we all needed to hear it. That was enough for me to get my ass here ASAP.

Before he has the opportunity to elaborate, the ring of Danger's phone echoes throughout the room. With a glance at the screen, he silences it only for the damn thing to start going off again right away.

"You need to get that, man? Might be your girlfriend." Joker taunts him.

"Fuck off, asshole." Danger fires back as he heads to the door. "Hey, Lexi. Kinda busy right now."

His feet become cement, freezing him in place in the middle of the room. "What the fuck. You sure?"

We all hold our breath, hanging on his every word like a bunch of busy bodies down at the diner.

"Alright, alright. I got it." Exasperation rings in his voice. "Where did they find the car?"

Foreboding steals in when the question drops like a bomb in the room. Uncharacteristic silence cloaks us all as the muffled voice rambles on for what feels like an eternity.

"Okay, thanks. Tell those idiots to stay the hell away until we get there." He issues the demand before ending the call. My bad feelings multiply when he zeroes right in on me.

"Prez. We gotta go. My neighbors found Demi's car totaled on the highway. Rocker and Bomber were knocked off their bikes. Lexi's brothers came across them unconscious. Their bikes are fucked to hell and back but they don't seem to be injured." He takes a breath before continuing.

"Those jackasses will keep people away until we get there to check on the scene."

"What about Demi?" Worry for my brother's wars with my need to keep my woman safe. Even though my main priority right now has to be Demi and her sister, I can't just turn off the leadership ingrained in me.

"No sign of either of the women." The admittance is precisely what I feared he would say.

"Fuck! Let's roll." All my brothers follow as I stand from my chair but Byte's next words stop me in my tracks.

"Prez. The Demon's President? He was seen with Sarah's ex." Knowing time is of the essence, he rushes on, ignoring the curses falling from Joker's lips. "He's how they know about Demi. Knew where to find her. He got in deep with them. Owes them a shit ton of money. Watch your back. I got a bad feeling about this. This has to be about more than just your woman."

With nothing but a nod, I make my way out the door with Joker hot on my heels. He's dying to get his hands on Sarah's ex and I can't say I blame him one bit.

We're chomping at the bit when we have to wait on Danger to lead the way. Even though we've been up to his cabin a few times, the damn place is so isolated it doesn't happen often enough that I know the roads as good as he does.

And fuck if this isn't a feeling I know well. Following instead of leading. I have no patience for the delay right now, riding his ass as we coast up the mountain. All sorts of horrific scenarios play out in my head.

Rolling up on the scene, a pretty brunette with straight dark hair all the way down to her ass crouches on the pavement next to Bomber. While her head may be tilted his way, her eyes are locked on Danger as the brother rolls to a stop at her side.

"Lexi." That's all the acknowledgement she gets before he turns to Bomber where he sits on the ground, leaning up against his mangled ride.

Fuck, there's no fixing that tangle of metal.

"What happened?" I ask the brother, taking in the road rash on his forearm and the side of his face.

I'm sorry, Prez. One minute we're rolling down the highway. The next thing I know, I'm on the ground. Fucking knocked out. Lexi and her brothers found us and woke our asses up." He admits with a grateful glance the woman's way.

"Where's Rocker?" I look around at what's left of the scene. The tangled mess of the brother's bikes. Demi's totaled car but no sign of Rocker.

"He took off with my brothers." It's Lexi that answers, straightening to her full height. She's tall for a woman, almost six feet if I had to guess.

"You let him leave with those idiots?" Danger seethes, stalking her way. "Dammit, if the people who took Prez's woman don't kill her, those moronic brothers of yours will finish the job."

The two glare each other down, a silent communication passing between them. A tension filled moment that makes me want to scream to the heavens. If looks could kill, Danger would be a pile of ash billowing smoke on the asphalt.

"Fuck, you let them go on purpose?" Danger demands in disbelief. "I told you to make sure they stay here, Lex."

"What were they supposed to do when it was *your* friend who stole their damn jeep?" She fires back. "They barely made the jump into the back before he took off like a bat out of hell."

"Took off where? Which way did they go?" I ask when she doesn't elaborate, deadly stare still aimed at my brother.

My heart pounds in my chest, each beat louder than the last, echoing the terror that grips my soul. The thought of Demi taken from this life is a nightmare I have no hope of escaping.

"Please, Lexi." I'm not above begging. The only thing that matters is finding Demi.

"That's my woman they have. These bastards are fucked up. If I don't find her-." I'm too choked up to continue. That horror reel of worst-case scenarios running on repeat through my head.

Images of her in danger. Her cries for help piercing the darkness, all gone unanswered by those heartless bastards. The fear is a constant, gnawing presence. A shadow looming larger with every second we stand around with our thumbs up our asses.

Helplessness is not a feeling I know well and I gotta say I don't like it one bit. Hands trembling, the world around me blurs, focus narrowed solely on the desperate need to find her. To save her from the unknown horrors her captors have in store for her and her sister.

The fear is raw, a visceral force, driving me to the brink of madness as I fight an overwhelming sense of dread.

Thankfully, the ring of a phone draws me back from those nightmares.

"Yeah? Where?" It must be Lexi's phone. Her voice the one that gives me a sliver of light in this dark and desolate situation.

I'm dying inside as I hang on her clipped side of the conversation. Those one-word responses not enough to give me any kind of hope. Any indication of what's happening.

"Okay. I'll bring them up there. Wait for us. Don't go in there half-cocked." She turns to face me after hanging up the call. Hand dropping to her side, she gives me my first silver lining.

"My brothers tracked them to a remote cabin that's been deserted for months. The owner has no desire to come back even though the place hasn't gotten much interest since he put it up for sale. I'll take you up there." She promises.

"Like hell, Lexi." Danger argues. "We don't know what we're walking into here. You're gonna stay the hell away."

The fearless woman gets right in his face. "You think I'm gonna leave my brothers out there alone? You? Those women? Like hell is that happening, Danger."

"Enough! Danger, step back." I break up their argument, no time for their shit. "We need all the help we can get. Lexi, I would appreciate you taking us up there."

"Prez-" Danger starts but I cut him off with a quickness.

"No, Danger. We're doing this my way." I tell him.

With a curse, he steps back out of respect, not looking at all happy about it.

I turn to Bomber, the brother has been silent through all of this.

"Bomb, how hurt are you?" I ask.

Struggling to his feet, he stands to his full height and stares me down with deadly intent. "I'm good, Prez. Just need my rifle."

I put my phone to my ear, the call answered right away. "Byte, get your ass out here with Bomb's rifle and more ammunition. We need your help, brother."

"On it, Prez." And then he's gone.

Even though standing around waiting is not my strong suit, there's not much more I can do until he gets here.

I turn to Joker, the brother who has been uncharacteristically quiet since we left the clubhouse. "You good to go, brother?"

"Yep, I got my head on straight, Prez. Nothing to worry about here." Thank fuck for that. The last thing I need is the volatile brother blowing this situation to hell and back.

"Lexi, tell us all about this cabin and the surrounding area." We need all the intel we can get and Lexi is our ace in the hole.

As she talks, a plan forms in my mind.

I'm on a mission and that mission is death.

Things move fast once Byte arrives on the scene. I issue my orders and we quickly mobilize to rain hell down on these bastards.

Hang on, Firecracker. I'm coming for you.

Chapter Forty

Demi

I wake in a fog, a powerful bass drum hammering away in my head. Lost and disoriented, I have no idea who I'm with. No idea where I am.

Wherever it is, it's pitch black in this bitch, no light penetrating to give me a clue.

Without my sight, I make use of my fingers, brushing around the scratchy surface beneath me. Which admittedly isn't far when quickly I realize my hands are tied up in knots at the small of my back. Real panic filters in as the bumpy movement of what I think is a car registers, slowly navigating some kind of rough terrain.

"Where the hell am I?" I ask no one in particular, struggling to recall how the hell I ended up here. The last memory I have was driving my car, Amy in the passenger seat as my babysitters escorted us on the road to the clubhouse.

My sister.

Where the hell is Amy? Because she sure as hell isn't in this tight space with me.

Mental paralysis sets in as I await whatever fate has in store.

Suddenly, the slam of a door echoes like a shot in the dark, followed quickly by a struggle as something or someone is dragged from the car. Stomping footsteps approach agonizing minutes later, a dark disturbance in the otherwise quiet of my surroundings.

Then the trunk flips open to reveal my worst nightmare.

Eyes squinting to adjust in the invading bright light, I gape at the last person in the world I hoped to see. "Dwight?"

Just my freakin' luck.

"Miss me?" The asshole towers over me, sneering down while yanking my arm to pull me from the car.

Heart racing, I lift my head as far as I can, desperate to catch sight of my sister. My eyes eat up the clearing we stand in but there's no sign of her out here.

"Where is my sister?" I demand with an eerie calm that belies my concern.

Dwight's eyes darken while the bastard's smile widens. "Don't worry about her. You should be more concerned about yourself right now."

"What the hell do you want from me?" I gotta buy myself some time here.

With thoughts of escape racing through my head, I force myself to keep a lid on my anger. At least until I can figure out a way to get my sister out of this mess. Or for Ryker to find us but from the remoteness of our location, I'm not so sure that's a realistic possibility at this point.

Either way, you can bet your ass once my baby sister is safe, all bets are off. This douchebag will get every dirty deed repaid tenfold and I feel no guilt about that.

Dwight leans in too close, revolting breath hot on my ear. "You'll find out soon enough." He whispers.

Suppressing the shiver that skates down my spine, I'll be damned if I give him any ammunition to stir up more fear. For way too long, he's had a hold on my life. It's time for that shit to stop.

I am so ready to take back my life.

The ring of his phone screams loud in the silence as we navigate the clearing to an old abandoned house. He answers it quickly with a curt, "Yeah?"

Ear hustler that I am, I strain to hear the conversation but only catch a few words. "Demon's MC... delivery... tonight."

My blood runs cold as a bigger picture forms. Dwight has a plan. Sell me and my sister for the Demon's. All the confirmation I need that the rumors of these bastard's dealing in human trafficking is true. Women specifically.

The notion of a stopover with them churns acid in my stomach. Dwight might be bad but there is no doubt in my mind I wouldn't survive an encounter with the rest of his twisted friends. There would be nothing left to sell to the highest bidder. It's a fate worse than death and I'll be damned if I'll let them force me to play that deadly game.

Focus girl! First things first, you need to find your sister.

"Where. Is. Amy?" Any plan to escape must start with finding her. There is no other option.

Fear eats away but not for myself. Amy is innocent in all this. I refuse to let her suffer for my dumbass mistakes.

Digging in my heels, I drag my feet as he forces me toward the rundown cabin ahead, instinctively knowing nothing good will happen in there. "I'm not going anywhere without my sister, asshole."

"Relax, *baby*." That mocking tone is a grate on my nerves. "I'm taking you to her."

All the fight leaves me, acquiescing for now. Once I get eyes on Amy, the first step of my plan can begin. As soon as I have one that is.

"Okay, okay. Relax. You're hurting me." I play up my injuries. Maybe if he thinks I'm impaired, it'll be to my advantage once I figure out how in the world I'm gonna get us out of this mess.

The douchebag just squeezes harder, tightening his hold to drag me up the rotting steps. Through the door we go and when my eyes adjust, I finally find my prize. My sister, while not exactly safe, appears unharmed so far.

Her bright blue eyes spit liquid fire above the gag in her mouth. A silent communication screaming her innermost thoughts on the piece of shit at my side.

If looks could kill, he'd be dead at my feet.

"Ahh, good. She's awake." Dwight says in delight.

"Amy! Are you okay?" I struggle to rip my arm from his grip but the effort is futile as he holds on tighter.

Let me go, asshole!" I continue my fight while gifting him a death glare, eyes full of all the hatred in my heart for this scumbag.

"What will you do for it, baby?" He leers closer. Way too close for my liking. "You gonna give me everything I want?"

I do nothing to hide my aversion as I lean as far away as I can.

"You want to save your sister? You know the Prez has a plan for her, and baby, you are not gonna like it." He shoots a lascivious look Amy's way with a lick of his lips. "So, I'll ask one more time. What will you do to save your sister? Save her from a life so full of pain you can't even imagine?"

A frisson of fear prickles all the way down to my toes. The fear I've lived with for over a year. Fear of the threat to my family – both blood and chosen – because of my stupidity.

Head whipping side to side, my sister begs me with her eyes. Silently screaming not to make such a fateful decision just for her. Consequences be damned, there is *nothing* I wouldn't do to keep her safe and the man standing way too close to my side knows that.

Unable to hold her gaze, my eyes drop in shame while I give him what he wants. "You know I'll do anything for her."

The triumph pouring from him churns my stomach. Self-disgust engulfs me at the fact I'm the one that delivered that satisfaction.

Focus on the now! You can unpack that shit when you get out of here.

Spinning me around, he releases my bonds.

"Good, then come here and kiss me." Arm snaking around my waist, he doesn't give me time to make the move on my own. Hauling me close, his dry lips press to mine, tongue forcing its way into my mouth.

Muffled screams from my sister reverberate in the background, mirroring my own horror as he molests my mouth.

Long agonizing seconds later, I get a reprieve to take a breath as he pulls back to issue his next ominous command. "Take off your shirt."

Thoughts racing, I see no way to refuse. No ideas come to mind. The only way forward is to continue this deadly game.

With no other choice, I pull my shirt from my jeans. Sliding the material up my ribcage and over my head, I drop it to stand in front of him in a sheer blue bra. Arms at my sides, I let him look his fill.

I will do whatever is necessary to save my sister from this same fate. No matter the cost. Because let's be real, we all know where this is headed.

The sadistic bastard wants to humiliate me. Hurt me in every way he can. By forcing my hand, making me put on this little performance in front of my own sister. He's winning this game, getting exactly what he wants. What turns him on.

Hand on my shoulder, he forces me to my knees, his other hand swiftly unbuttoning his jeans. "You know what to do. Show me how much of a whore he's turned you into."

There's no possible way to hide the hatred on my face.

"Tsk, tsk, Demi. Remember who you're doing this for." He reminds me with a pointed look Amy's way. As if I could forget that little fact.

"You don't want to do this? I'm sure your sister is dying to take your place. Do you think she'll do whatever it takes to keep you safe?"

Gaze dropping in shame, I avoid all eye contact as Amy's screams skyrocket despite the gag in her mouth.

Just when I build up the courage to follow his order, what feels like a nuclear bomb rocks the earth beneath my knees. Bells ringing in my ears, I whip around to see what the hell just happened.

My jaw drops.

Oh shit. A bomb *did* go off.

The entire front half of the cabin is just *gone*.

Blown to smithereens.

With debris raining down, two men take up the space where the door once stood.

At least, I assume they're men. I can't say for sure what with the hillbilly doomsday look they have going on.

Really, the explosion must have seriously affected my sanity. Has my mind playing tricks on me.

Confusion.

Perplexity.

Disbelief.

Alternate universe shit going on around here.

What can only be described as homemade riot gear adorns their bodies, complete with hand stitched chain mail peeking out from cast iron plates hanging over their chests. Tactical pants and combat boots complete the inconceivable look.

Gas masks conceal what I'm sure are diabolical smiles as they high five through rubber gloves before splitting off with a bow to flank the man I love as he races up the steps.

I knew in my heart he would come for me but my relief is short lived. Anger fills his face when he takes in my position.

Heart pounding in shame, embarrassment flames in my cheeks at the scene he walked into.

"Take your fucking hands off her." With that one sentence, my fear vaporizes like smoke in the sky. Calm tranquility sags every muscle in my body when that achingly familiar voice joins the ringing in my ears.

Chapter Forty-One

Ryker

We race to the cabin high up in the mountains of Thunder Ridge Falls, Danger leading the way with Lexi at his back.

She motions our little caravan to a stop on the side of the road and climbs off the bike.

"We have to walk from here." Accepting her explanation, I nod and step to the side so she can move ahead of the pack.

Trees tower above us, branches gently swaying in the wind. The crunch of our boots on fallen leaves the only sound that breaks the eerie silence.

The air is crisp and cold, biting into our skin as we push our way through the dense foliage.

Rounding the edge of the trees, a sight that will haunt me for the rest of my days stands right up ahead. In the middle of a clearing in front of a cabin, Rocker is locked in a heated exchange with two men in fucking homemade battle gear. That is until one of the men loses patience and pulls a *pipe bomb* out of his pants as he forces his way past my brother.

"What the fuck?" I yell, breaking into a full out run. "No!"

But it's too late. The idiot launches the makeshift bomb at the door with deadly accuracy.

The front of the cabin explodes right before my eyes, rocking me back from the force of the blast.

Shaking the fog from my head, I push right back to my feet, pulling my gun from my side as I rush inside what's left of the cabin. Fury burns the ice in my veins at the scene laid out in front of me. My woman forced cruelly to her knees at the feet of this bastard.

Dwight.

DeLuca is nowhere in sight.

A surging tidal wave of anger obliterates the walls of my self-control. Every muscle in my body coils tight, ready to spring into action. The sight of his smug face only adds fuel to my fire.

"Get away from her." I growl, voice low and dangerous. In direct contrast to the battle cry crashing through my chest with every beat of my heart.

"Or what?" The asshole taunts me, eyes gleaming with malice, a smirk playing on his lips.

I take a step forward, fists clenched at my sides.

"Or you *will* regret it." I promise, voice steady and unwavering.

The asshole's smirk starts to falter in the face of the anger blasting from my eyes.

But it's not anywhere near enough to quell the storm raging inside me. The need to protect my woman – to make this piece of shit pay for his audacity. It is an all-consuming beast seething within, no room left for doubt or hesitation.

My gun cocked and ready, I hold my arm steady. Barrel aimed right at his head, daring him to test me.

Praying that he does.

"Come here, Demi." Keeping my eyes on the bastard, I catch her rise to her feet out of the corner of my eye but the damn woman doesn't do as I ask.

Instead, she steps right up and lodges her knee in his junk with enough force to drop him to his knees. "Asshole!" She spits in his face.

Then she moves quickly to her sister, untying her gag and working through the knots on her wrists.

Once free, Demi wraps her arm around Amy, no thought to the fact she's in nothing but a bra in front of this bastard.

"Rocker, get them out of here." I issue the order, keeping my eyes locked on the dead man dry heaving without an ounce of pity.

Following my order, Rocker surrounds both the women, big body a shield as he hustles the duo to safety.

Once they're clear of the building, I let the beast off its leash.

"Dwight, I assume?" I ask the man on his knees. A chilling smile gracing my lips as the realization of the desolation of his situation penetrates at last.

"You're a dead man, Ryker." He gasps out through his pain. "You have no idea what my club is capable of."

The false bravado falls flat in the face of my deadly intent.

"I don't think so, asshole. You have no idea who you fucked with but you'll learn soon enough." I promise him.

"Prez, we gotta get out of here." Bomber calls from my back.

He's not worth the time I'm wasting on him.

My woman is my priority. So much more important than this piece of shit.

"Come get this shit stain ready to move. You know where to take him." Now that the drama is over, I need to lay hands on my woman. Reassure myself she really is alive and unharmed. It's the only possible way to tame the beast.

Slipping back down the steps, my long-legged strides carry me right to her. My heart breaks at the wary look on her face and that is just not acceptable. Walking right into her, I wrap my arms around her sides, lifting until she can wrap her legs around my waist. She clings to me as tight as I do her, not a bit of space between us.

Face buried in her long hair, I let the control slip as a ground shaking shudder moves through the entirety of my body, inhaling the sugar and spice scent I thought I would never experience again. The unique scent of Demi intertwined with a cloud of smoke from the explosion that took ten years off my life.

"Baby." My voice breaks on that one little word but she knows me so well. Knows just how to conquer the beast raging within.

"I'm okay, Big Guy. I'm okay. I knew you would come for me." With her face buried in my neck, she soothes me, her soft breath cooling the fire burning just beneath the surface of my skin.

Not one word is necessary. She lends me her strength to tame my erratic emotions, get them back under control. This woman knows exactly what I need. When I'm too weak to be strong, she takes on my burden, fighting the demons right beside me.

"Prez, we really need to go. The Sheriff is on his way. Lexi and I will stay here but if you want to handle this ourselves, he needs to get gone." Danger warns.

Demi lifts her head, blue eyes piercing right to the heart of me. "I'm okay, Ryker. Go take care of him. I'll be waiting when you're done."

Chapter Forty-Two

Demi

"Stop sulking." My sister reprimands. "You are a badass and that is not what we do."

So much for sympathy from my baby sister. That shit lasted as long as it took to get us home, showered and wrapped up in our pajamas. Then she took the bull by the horns and made me talk through it all.

As I do indeed sit here sulking, I gotta say it was the right call to make. She got me out of my head and my emotions locked down tight before Ryker returned that night.

Covered in what I knew to be blood, he walked in the house, took my hand in silence and all but dragged me to the shower where I washed it all away with the softest of touches as he cried into my hair. My own heart breaking, I held him close while he let all his pent up fear wash down the drain.

After our shower, we fell into bed and clung to one another, not a stitch of clothing between us. I woke to the sun shining high in the sky, wrapped up in his arms just as tight as when I fell asleep.

As I laid there in the soothing silence, the calming rise and fall of Ryker's chest under my cheek brought comfort and contentment in the otherwise silent morning.

That is until he woke up and started treating me like a porcelain doll. For every move I made, he hovered all the same, not letting me out of his sight for even a second. I ultimately called in reinforcements and promptly kicked his ass out of the house for a little breather and a whole lotta scheming.

In my heart, I knew Ryker would come for me that day and I'm okay with the fact that I did what I needed to survive until he showed. Unfortunately, he doesn't feel the same. The waves of guilt rolling off his back have been a noose tightening around both our necks this past week. Suffocating in ways I never thought possible.

And an unacceptable byproduct of that guilt – he's afraid to touch me. To give me what I so desperately need. A return to normalcy, in all ways but he hasn't taken the hint.

If not for my sister, I would be climbing the walls. Screams echoing through the halls every time he treated me like a porcelain doll and I am so over it.

It's time for that crap to stop.

As infuriating as the last week has been, I know his overprotectiveness comes from a place of love. That is the only reason I've given him a pass this long but that ends now.

First, though, I need to come up with a plan to knock him off his feet. Literally, because I'm feeling a little frisky and he's the only one with the power to scratch my itch. Subtle hints haven't worked so it's time to pull out the big guns.

Now here I sit, surrounded by all the girls I call sisters, plotting ways to beat some sense into the man that holds my heart.

"I can't keep living like this. I get it, he's worried about me but treating me like I'm breakable doesn't help a damn thing. I need him to see me as his partner, not someone in constant need of his protection. At least, not *only* in need of his protection." I vent my frustration to my girls.

"You could ask him to take you on a ride. Those always get Mac's motor revving." My bestie suggests, slowly nursing her first glass of wine.

I shake my head at her idea. "I gotta get him to stop treating me like I'm made of glass before he'll even listen to that idea."

She's a lightweight, so I'll give her a pass until she consumes a little more wine before even considering her suggestions.

I turn expectant eyes to my girl Sarah for her turn at the metaphorical whiteboard.

"Umm. Why don't you just sit down and talk to him about it?" Her suggestion is hesitant and a little too mature for my liking.

The snort from my baby sister echoes that thought.

"Sorry, girl. You're demoted from brain-stormer to wine girl. Still a super important contribution though. Gotta keep the vino flowing." Apology fills my smile while simultaneously wiggling my glass in her direction.

This requires some serious scheming here and my girl isn't quite up to the task just yet.

She doesn't seem offended though. With a shrug, she downs the rest of the blood red liquid in her glass.

I need to get my man back.

Metaphorically speaking.

He's here but he's not *here* if you know what I mean.

"Play a little game. Pretend to be a hooker. Dress all out and pick him up outside the club." Sarah, the poor girl, chokes on that gulp of wine she just took at the suggestion from my sister.

At least it didn't project out this time. Red wine is a bitch to get out of the furniture.

"Only if you want to give him a heart attack." My bestie chimes in with a little common sense.

I have to admit that one surprised even me and I taught my sister all her tricks.

"What? Don't look at me like that. I've learned things since you moved out here." She defends her outlandish idea.

Guess she learned a few new "tricks".

"Please tell me you haven't done that before. Do you know how dangerous that could be?" It's not often I pull the big sister card but damn the thought of my baby sister on the streets picking up a man? Aside from the danger, that is so not an image I want in my head.

"Hey, don't knock it til you try it. I got all kinds of ideas to spice up your love life." She defends herself.

"*Anyway.*" I table that topic for now but you can bet your ass we'll be revisiting it in the future.

"So, we need something that falls between date night and prostitution." I mumble as I stop to think.

There has to be some kind of middle ground here.

"Or, you know, you could just be yourself. I think all you really need to do is show up all dolled up and give him hell. That'll knock him off his feet. It is how you hooked him in the first place." Kate says. "I could get Mac to give everyone a heads up to clear the place out after you get him all hot and bothered."

Hmm. Maybe my bestie isn't half bad at this after all.

"You know what girl, I think you're on to something." Gotta give credit where credit is due.

"Okay." Even my sister agrees with this tamer suggestion. "So, what are you going to wear? You have to have something sexy in your closet. The less fabric the better. Maybe a cross between hooker and club goer." She snickers.

"You know, I think I have the perfect little getup." My smile laced with deviousness, I jump to my feet and race up the stairs.

There in the back of the closet hangs the cutest sapphire blue dress I've been saving for just the right occasion.

Two pieces but not really much fabric between the two. The top is more of a strapless bandeau style. The skirt so small it barely covers my ass with thin crisscrossing straps to connect the two rounds out the dress.

This is just the thing to snag the Big Guy's attention.

"Amy! Get your ass up here and help me get ready!" I yell down from the top of the stairs.

It's not just Amy that comes running at my summons. My two friends are hot on her heels as excited girlie chatter explodes through our little love den. AKA the master bedroom. The place where a different kind of magic is about to happen.

"Okay. Sit down and let me get to work, Sis." Amy takes charge.

An hour and a lot of vino later, I float across the room to the floor length mirror to check out her handiwork and let me tell you she did not disappoint. I am absolutely blown away with her talent. She nailed the exact look I was going for – temptation with a side of slutty – and I gotta say I have never felt so sexy.

"You're welcome." She says while buffing her nails on her chest, not an ounce of shame in her confidence.

Prepared for war, I slip black strappy heels on my feet, tying the leather around my calves after wrapping them up and around my ankles.

"Alright. Let's get this show on the road." I'm ready for war and my man isn't gonna know what hit him.

Ready or not, here I come Big Guy.

Chapter Forty-Three

Ryker

My head like an anvil weighing down my shoulders, I lose the hard fought battle, dropping it to rest on the back of my chair in exhaustion. My bed is calling my name but the evil woman I love won't let me go home just yet.

It's been a fuck of a long week. Interrogating Demi's asshole ex, Bomber has been able to get all sorts of intel from him. The man is deadly when he zeroes in on a target. Don't ask me how, his ways are his secrets to tell.

When he eventually got every last detail about the Demon's plans in this town, we called in the Sheriff to pass the intel on. He took it from there, calling in the State Police and shutting those vile bastards down once and for all. The women they held rescued, both locally and back in California.

The fact they had the same fate in store for my woman signed Dwight's death warrant. You bet your ass he'll get what's coming as soon as he recovers from Bomber's administrations.

The only loose end is Sarah's ex. The slippery bastard escaped our clutches once again. He's like a fucking cat but his lives are running out.

Joker has been on a rampage, tearing through everything we have to try to dig up his whereabouts. Surly as all hell, the only time he's halfway human is the time he spends with Sarah and the kids at night.

Danger has been conspicuously absent the last seven days. Probably dealing with those crazy lunatics who live a little too close to home.

If I wasn't so caught up in tying up loose ends and thanking my lucky stars that Demi is safe, I would have shot those idiots myself for putting her in danger. Still might if our paths ever cross again.

For now, they're Danger's problem but don't think I didn't give him a warning to keep them as far from me as possible. If I never see those degenerates again it'll be too soon.

"Prez, you need to get the hell out here!" I sigh at the pound of Mac's fist on my door.

"Fuck." I'm tired as fuck and this shit never ends. "Okay, okay. I'm coming." Hands on the arms of my chair, I push my tired ass up and drag my feet across the floor.

"What is it?" From the look on Mac's face when I swing open the door, I'm not sure I'm gonna like whatever he has to say.

"Come on, man. This is something better seen than heard." Intrigued by the vague comment, I follow him down the hall.

What I find when I clear the hallway sets my blood on fire.

Dancing in the middle of the room, my Firecracker sways sensually for all the world to see. In two scraps of fabric barely covering her tits and ass, she leaves nothing to the imagination as her body gyrates to the sensual pounding bass. My neglected cock weeps at the sight. I can do nothing but watch the erotic show she's putting on just for me but a nudge from Mac reminds me I'm not the only man in the room. Swinging around, I snarl at a couple of visitors too stupid to look away.

"Get the fuck out!" My order echoes over the music, all focus narrowly locked on the beauty in front of me. When I don't hear enough movement for my liking, I reluctantly tear my eyes away, narrowing in on every motherfucker in the room. "Now!"

"Go get her before she starts a riot, man." With a laugh and a slap on the back, he starts herding everyone out the door. Mac's words are all the impetus I need to propel my ass across the room until I'm standing right in front of her.

The hypnotic woman must sense me, her eyelids slowly rising as her hands caress down her ribcage. Over the skin exposed by the missing fabric of her dress to sensually map her hips in the way my own burn to do. I'm drawn to her like a moth to a flame, moving forward until I'm all up in her space.

In the now empty room, I wrap my arm around her waist, drawing her generous curves flush to my hard plains.

"What are you doing, Firecracker?" My voice is a croak, desire choking the life out of me, no room left to breathe.

From the look in her eyes, she's suffering the same affliction as me.

"I was feeling a little lonely, Big Guy. Figured I'd come see what kind of trouble I could stir up." Her words are a purr, rumbling right to the heart of me.

Desire slams me so hard, I have to lock my knees to remain on my feet. "Oh, yeah? I'm afraid to ask what devious scheme you came up with."

Her first real smile of the week lifts the weight off my shoulders. This woman is strong. I was a dumbass for treating her like she's fragile.

"Hmm. I'm not sure you deserve what I have in mind, Big Guy." She sasses while winding her arms around my neck. "You've been an ass this week."

"Then who the hell did you get all dolled up for?" I ask in mock outrage.

The jealousy though? That shit is real at even the thought of any other asshole laying eyes on her when she walked in here looking like every man's wet dream.

"What if I just did it for myself?" Her fingers slide into my hair, massaging away at the tension in the back of my neck.

There is no controlling the groan that escapes me, so I don't even try.

"Then I'm just the lucky bastard that gets to benefit and show my appreciation." I could give a fuck if she denies it but she did this all for me.

To pull my head straight out of my ass.

"Yeah? What kind of benefits do you think you deserve?" The sass in her voice turns my cock to steel.

My hands roam her body, slipping over the soft skin exposed on her sides on the way to her ass. I can't help but give those luscious globes a squeeze where they play peekaboo with the hem of her skirt.

"I'm a selfish man, baby. I want them all." I give her my truth.

Every day with this woman is a gift and I'll be damned if I waste another second.

Unfortunately, the vixen in my arms has other ideas. Shoving me away, she doubles down on her erotic performance, tempting me closer as she glides across the floor. A dog on a leash, I follow with pride until she shoves me onto a stool at the bar.

When I reach for her automatically, she admonishes me with a shake of a finger in my face. "No touching. Just watch."

I snort out a laugh. "That's like asking the sun not to rise, Firecracker."

I may have some long ago experience following orders in service to my country but that is not the case with this woman. She holds the key to my heart and I'm not ashamed to admit it.

With a sultry wink thrown over her shoulder, she backs her ass right up into my lap. Swiveling and grinding, she knows precisely how to wind me up.

Thank God, I kicked everyone out of the club.

I would have killed any motherfucker peeping on this show.

My resolve to keep my hands to myself lasts but a minute before they're on the move with a mind of their own. Gripping her sinful flesh, I pull her all the way down to meet my bucking hips, grinding my cock hard right where he wants to go.

"This what you wanted, baby? This the endgame of your sexy little show?"

Her moan is all the answer I need as I sink my teeth straight into her neck. Licking and biting, I leave my mark with an unhealthy dose of possession.

"Hey, buddy. Hands off the merchandise." She continues the charade, swatting at my hands but her body gives her away.

Her ass presses down hard as she chases the pleasure only I can provide before slipping away just far enough to turn face to face. Then the little minx swings a leg up for leverage to climb on my lap.

Panting breaths mingled, we're eye to eye, seeing straight into the other's soul.

I see my future in that one look. All wrapped up in this sexy little package.

I wrap a hand in her hair, twisting and tightening until her mouth meets mine.

Her surrender is sweet with the first press of my lips, nipping and sucking she chases my mouth until I give her what she needs.

Covering her mouth completely, no battle of wills is necessary. Tongues thrusting and retreating, the control she relinquishes is as arousing as everything else about this woman.

Where in all other aspects of our relationship she stands toe to toe with me, when it comes to our sex life, she happily surrenders the power. After a bit of a struggle because, of course, she wouldn't be my Firecracker if she didn't make me work for it a little.

I slip her flimsy excuse for panties to the side, release my cock from my jeans and then slide into heaven.

It takes an embarrassingly short time to reach the pinnacle. Clinging tight to one another, we come together with my cock buried deep and my fingers on her clit to get her there with me.

We're a panting mess of flesh and sweat as we come down from the high, recovering from the best sex of my life.

"We good?" Face buried in my neck, her question is a welcome breeze over my sweat slickened skin.

"Perfect, baby." I answer with a brush of my lips to her hair and one last squeeze to her ass.

"No, not perfect." She denies with a laugh. "Perfect is boring. Perfectly imperfect."

I let loose a bark of a laugh but when she lifts her face, I'm in awe of all the love in her soul shining through from her eyes. "I love you, Big Guy."

"Love you too baby." I promise her.

Then I pick her up and carry her to my room and show her exactly how much. My patience for the drive home no match for my out of control need for this woman.

She's right, we may not be perfect but we are perfect for each other. I can't wait for whatever shenanigans are in store for me with this woman at my side.

Chapter Forty-Four

Demi

The day has finally come to see my bestie's dream transform into a reality. Here we stand at the opening of her safe haven and I can't help but bask in a proud mama bear moment as she takes center stage with happy tears in my eyes.

My bestie is about as far from an attention seeker as you can get. Something we have in common.

I know, crazy right? Me not seeking the spotlight?

But that is all about my outrageousness, not at all about accolades.

Believe me, there's a big difference between the two.

Back to my bestie though. Her radiant smile shines like a beacon from where she stands in front of the doors of the renovated hotel.

Scissors in hand, she readies herself to cut the symbolic red ribbon decorating the entrance. A smile of my own spreads my lips just as wide. I am absolutely bursting at the seams, words not enough to convey the depth of pride in my friend.

As she cuts the ribbon, sandwiched between her man and Joker, I stick my fingers in my mouth, giving the loudest, proudest whistle in the history of the world.

Throwing her head back in laughter, she knows exactly who it is making a spectacle of the day. In her usual fashion, she accepts me as I am. Head shaking at my brazenness with a smile on her face despite the blush staining her cheeks.

With his arm wrapped around me, Ryker pulls me into his side. "You about done embarrassing your friend, Firecracker?"

"Never! She makes it way too easy." His laughter echoes mine as he presses a kiss to my upturned lips when I lift my face to his.

"Ready to go celebrate?" Is that a serious question? He knows I am so ready to honor the shit out of my friend.

"Hell yes!" I nod my agreement, ready to get back to the clubhouse and get this party started.

Life has gone somewhat back to normal after my impromptu visit to the clubhouse a month ago. Since then, while Ryker hasn't fully let go of his overprotective tendencies, he is talking things through when he gets close to the edge. It's all I can ask for and exactly what I need.

Sliding onto the back of his motorcycle, I cling to him as he revs the engine and pulls out on the highway. His men fall in formation with him leading the pack, a silent recognition of the power of his leadership. Of the fact these men will follow him anywhere, no questions asked.

By the time we roll to a stop in front of the clubhouse, my body is vibrating with all kinds of excitement as I hop off the bike. This is the first party we've thrown since all the crap went down with my ex and I am so ready to let loose.

Much to the chagrin of my friend, cheers drown out the bass pounding through the speakers as she precedes us into the club. The ladies have been busy little bees. With Jade leading the charge, the room has been completely transformed just in time for the celebration.

Streamers and balloons drape from the ceiling, complete with a strobe light flashing a rainbow of colors over us all. A huge banner hangs front and center in honor of my friend and I have to say Jade did an amazing job.

Admittedly, she may have gone a little overboard but I can't deny I probably would have done the same exact thing.

Now that the guest of honor has arrived, the ladies converge on the dance floor. On her way to join them, Jade snags my bestie's hand and pulls her into the fold. With a shake of his head, Mac continues on to talk to the other men at the bar.

Pressing a quick kiss to Ryker's lips, I prance over to support my friend. Head thrown back in glee, I sidle up to my bestie giving her a quick hip check to get her ass shaking.

Even though another blush burns her cheeks, she gets the message and starts getting down.

For what feels like hours, we dance around my friend. Gyrating and swaying until Mac and Ryker intercede to drag us off the dance floor but the sight of the two women standing right inside the door stops me in my tracks.

"Mom? Bianca? Is everything okay? What are you doing here?" I ask, rushing over to meet them at the edge of the dance floor.

"Ryker invited us. We wanted to see you." Surprisingly, that comes from Bianca. Her words freeze me in place, suspended in the motion of reaching for my mom.

I gape at my sister, probably looking like a fish out of water, complete with lips flapping. At a loss for words because damn that hit me out of left field.

"Really? You wanted to see *me*?" I feel like I'm in the twilight zone.

Don't get me wrong, I love my family. All of them, but Bianca and I have *never* been close.

"Yes, Demi. I wanted to see you. That man of yours called. Had some enlightening truths to lay on me." She says sheepishly.

Taking a deep breath, she continues to blow me away. "I'm sorry for the way I've treated you. I didn't know how to connect with you. I think it's obvious how different we are and I pushed you away because of it when I should have been trying to bridge that gap. Despite our differences."

I have no idea what to say. Honestly, I'm speechless right now.

I know, it surprises me too.

Thankfully, in her achingly familiar way, mom jumps in. She pulls me close while wrapping her other arm around Bianca. "I love you, girls. All I've ever wanted was for you to have a close relationship."

Bianca pulls back with a hesitant smile and a shy look stamped all over her face. "I'm good with that if you are?"

Wow, I can't even right now. Still feels like an alternate reality in here.

"Yeah? I'd like that too." I agree with optimism and a healthy dose of caution. It's going to take a lot more than one quick conversation to turn this relationship around but I'm willing to give it a try.

"So how long are you here for and why didn't anyone tell me you were coming?" I ask only half joking.

While mom has recovered for the most part, she's still a little slower. Not as strong, physically, at least.

"Well, that depends on you, baby." Mom says with a smile. "Ryker offered to let us stay as long as we want and we really want to be a part of your life here. We miss you."

Tears gather on my lashes at the sincerity of her words.

"Wow, okay. Um, if that's what you want. I would love to have you stay. For as long as you want. I missed you both too." Strangely enough I can say it with complete honesty about the two of them.

With a wink, Mom asks, "So are you going to introduce us to your friends? And that man of yours? We haven't met in person yet and I really would like to thank him."

Glancing around, I see he's conspicuously absent now.

"He was here a minute ago." I answer while scanning the room for the big guy.

Before I get a chance to go hunt the sneaky man down, Amy pops up out of nowhere and wraps her arms around Mom. "Mom! Bianca! What are you doing here?"

She shoots a wide-eyed look my way from over her shoulder.

I give her a shrug, a silent communication I'm as shocked to see them as she is.

"Amy, sweetheart! We missed you and Demi. Ryker called to let us know the situation with Dwight was over and invited us to visit." She says. "Since the threat is over, we thought it would be the perfect time to come see you both."

Well, well. The big guy sure has been a sneaky, sneaky little thing. Going behind my back to talk all kinds of things out without my knowledge.

Speaking of, I do another sweep around the room. Eventually, I catch sight of him walking back into the room from the hallway to his office.

"There he is. I'll be right back." I don't wait for a response, scooting across the room to intercept him.

Wary emerald eyes watch me with a boatload of caution as I beeline right to him. "Baby-"

"Don't you baby me. What did you do?" I ask, stepping right up into his personal space, finger stabbing into his chest.

"You're mad?" He asks. "I thought you missed your mom."

"I did." I concede. "I do."

"Then what are you mad about, Firecracker? You look like you're ready to blow." The jerk presses his luck, calling me on my shit.

"Dammit, don't take the wind out of my sails." I whine like a little brat. "I'm mad at you! What did you say to my sister?"

I know, I know. I am *so* acting like a child but I can't seem to pump the brakes here.

The scales have shifted between me and my oldest sister and I'm not sure how I feel about that. More so, I'm a little bit afraid to trust the change.

Snaking his arm around my neck, he yanks me close, leaning down until we're face to face. "I want you to be happy, Demi. That includes having a good relationship with *both* of your sisters. How were you supposed to do that with thousands of miles between you two?"

With a ghost of a kiss across my lips, he turns me around, propelling me forward with a slap on the ass. "Come on, Firecracker. Introduce me to your family."

"Don't think I'm gonna forget about this, you little schemer." I sass him over my shoulder even as I follow his order and drag him their way. "I'll find a way to get even."

Throwing his head back in laughter, he says. "Baby, I'm looking forward to it."

See? This is why I love the big guy. He gets me. Accepts me, flaws and all. Even going so far as encouraging my behavior as outrageous as it might be on occasion.

With huge smiles gracing both our faces, we arrive back at their sides. Where without an ounce of hesitation, I introduce my family to the love of my life.

Once that's done, I lead them to the bar to meet everyone else. Surprisingly, they both fit right in. Mom holds court, settling in with my Frostown family like she's been here for years. Captivating them all with the stories of my youth.

And that's how the rest of the night goes.

We drink. We dance. We laugh.

We have a blast.

Even Bianca – who somewhere along the way pulled the stick out of her ass – is actually enjoying herself with all of us ladies.

Just one more thing to thank Jade for. She shoved a shot glass in her hand and wouldn't take no for an answer. While Bianca certainly hasn't kept up with her – nor has she tried – she truly seems to be enjoying herself with my chosen family.

A little before midnight, Ryker draws me back to the dance floor to sway to the slow pounding beat.

I have to remind myself to keep things PG with my mom in the room. Resting my cheek on his chest, I sigh in contentment at the perfection of this man.

"You happy, baby?" He asks softly, tangling his fingers in the long strands of my hair.

I raise my head to gift him with the goofiest smile in history. "Of course. Things couldn't be better but don't think everything is going to magically change with me and my sister. It'll take time to get past all our crap."

His answering laugh takes all my breath away. So much so, I lean up on my toes, unable to resist those irresistible lips. I slip down the slope into PG-13 territory for a scorching hot kiss before I remember my mom is still in the room.

When I try to slip away, he doesn't let me get far, holding me in place with his hand tangled in my hair. "I love you, Demi."

"Love you too, Big Guy." Heart swelling with happiness, I intertwine our fingers to lead him back to the table, enjoying the rest of the night with my family.

Life may not be perfect. I may have a long way to go with my older sister. Ryker and I may have some growing to do together.

But in this magical moment, none of that matters. There's not a damn thing that can dampen my happiness right now.

Our future is bright and I am so ready for all the adventures to come with this man at my side.

Epilogue

Demi

As I relax in my chair, the fading sunlight gives way to an abundance of stars in the sky, their sparkly reflections dancing over the waves rolling up on the lakeside shore.

But that isn't the best part. No, what makes the night perfect is the man sprawled out blissfully on the porch by my side. *Our* porch since he got his way and moved me in permanently.

The devious man admitted he had no intention of letting me go once he got me in his space and I am so not mad about it.

The last six months since everything went down with my ex have been the best of my life. All thanks to the man lounging next to me.

He's been my rock as I navigate my trauma. As much as I tried to convince myself the whole thing didn't affect me, that wasn't actually the case.

On this long road to acceptance, he's been right there by my side, holding me up when I was too weak to do it on my own. I can honestly say I wouldn't be in the mental headspace I am now if not for him.

His support, his patience. His *love*.

Those were the things that got me through. The things that mattered the most.

Surprisingly, my sister Amy has settled here in Frostown without a single misstep. What I thought would turn her away is just the thing she says she needs. A slowdown from the rat race of California.

She moved into the apartment above the bakery, much to Rocker's vexation. The big baby threw the mother of all fits when she made that declaration. I still have no idea what the hell is going on with those two.

All I can say is he gets a warning from me every chance I get. Sometimes Ryker has to reel me back from my threatening stance.

221

Okay. Okay. Most of the time but what can I say. That's my baby sister he's got a thing for.

At least, I think it's a thing. I can't say with a hundred percent certainty what with the way they dance around each other like a choreographed play.

Whatever it is, I still don't like it. I don't want to see my sister hurt and while he might be infatuated for the moment, I've seen the way these men go through women. The thought of him toying with my sister boils my blood even though Ryker assures me that's not how it is at all.

Even my relationship with my older sister has turned a corner. We're certainly not as close as I am with Amy but the barbs aren't as biting as they once were. When we stopped talking *at* each other and really started listening to one another, we realized we have so much more in common than either of us could imagine.

I think it shocked the heck out of us both.

She comes to visit now. Both her and Mom are here more often than not. Even going so far as considering a permanent move in the not-so-distant future.

That'll definitely be another test of our relationship. Infrequent small doses are a whole lot different than interacting on the daily but I'm doing my best to keep my promise to Ryker. To be positive and open minded with her.

Only time will tell on that front. For now, I'm enjoying the hell out of the life I'm building with this man of mine.

"What's going through that pretty little head of yours, Firecracker?" The love of my life brings me back to the present. Lifting my hand to his lips, he presses a kiss to the back of my knuckles.

"Just how perfect this is. Being here with you." I admit.

From the smile lighting his face, that is exactly what he wanted to hear.

"Hey, don't get a big head over there, Big Guy." I sass. "That could always change if you start slacking."

I'm a filthy little liar. This man is the center of my world and he sees right through my bullshit.

Still, he indulges my game. "I'll keep that in mind, baby."

"You want something to drink?" Empty beer bottle in hand, he moves to stand.

"Stay there. I'll get it." Instead of answering his question, I get up to fetch him another. Best to make the trek myself, lest I give myself away by forgoing a drink.

After a stop in the bathroom, I grab the bottle from the fridge and head back to the porch, freezing in shock with one foot through the door at the transformation in front of me.

Ryker was a busy little bee in the few minutes I was gone. Candlelight dances over every inch of the porch, casting soft shadows into the dark night beyond.

But all that fades to the background in a heart stopping second because the man who holds my heart is down on one knee in the middle of it all.

My feet are frozen.

My lungs are seized.

My heart stops beating mere seconds before taking off in a galloping race in my chest.

Oh. My. God.

"Come here, baby." My feet unfreeze at the command in his voice, carrying me right to him with not an ounce of hesitation.

"I won't bite." He teases. "At least not yet."

The joke releases the seizure of my lungs, air whooshing in as I draw lifesaving oxygen into my body.

"I love you, Demi. The world is brighter with you in my life and I can't imagine it any other way. You make my days brighter. I never know what to expect and I love that about you. I want you by my side forever in this amazing life we've built here. Will you marry me, Firecracker?"

My hand flies to my mouth as I gaze down at him in wonder but I can't help making him sweat a little bit before saying yes.

"It's a good thing you plan to make an honest woman out of me. Otherwise, the gossips down at the diner would have plenty of new fodder as soon as my belly pops out."

It takes but a minute for my words to sink in and when they do the brightest smile I have ever seen brightens his face.

"A baby?" His voice fills with wonder before that smile morphs to one full of male pride as he caresses my stomach in awe.

"You might want to dial back that smug look right there, Big Guy, or I'll tell everyone who will listen we're having a shotgun wedding." I tease him.

The laugh that bursts free sets my body on fire, but the soft kiss pressed to my still flat belly is what melts my heart.

This man.

He is by far the best man I've ever met and I'm the lucky bitch that gets to call him mine.

You better believe I'll shout that shit to the rooftops while flashing my swollen belly for all the world to see.

"I want to spend the rest of my life with you, Demi." He says. "The baby? That's just icing on the cake of this perfect life we have."

And like I always do, I remind him. "Perfectly imperfect, Big Guy. Now give me my ring."

He does just that then he surges to his feet, spinning in a circle while kissing the hell out of me.

This is the life. It may not be perfect but it's exactly what I need.

THE END

Thank you for reading Demi and Ryker's story, I hope you love them as much I do! Good, bad or ugly, reviews are greatly appreciated to keep me honest as I continue this journey.

Want more of the Broken Souls? Sign up for my newsletter for a sneak peek of Danger's story in a loosely related new series!

Also by Terri Marie Pemberton

Broken Souls Motorcycle Club
Ryker's War (Broken Souls Motorcycle Club)

Standalone
Mac's Choice

Watch for more at https://www.facebook.com/people/Terri-Marie-Pemberton-Author/61564954880361/.

About the Author

Dear Readers,

Thank you so much for reading my story! I hope you loved it as much as I love my couples as their stories come to life. It's not easy putting my thoughts and emotions into words and then sharing them with others. Knowing that you are out there enjoying my work makes it all worthwhile.

Like everything in life, this is a constant journey of growth, so please keep me honest.

Connect with me on Goodreads and Facebook to let me know what you think!

All the love

Terri Marie Pemberton

Read more at https://www.facebook.com/people/Terri-Marie-Pemberton-Author/61564954880361/.